GOD BLESS JOHN WAYNE

Kinky Friedman, former leader of the band The Texas Jewboys, lives on a ranch in the Texas Hill Country with two dogs, two cats and one armadillo. He is the author of nine internationally acclaimed mystery novels and six country music albums.

D1635540

KINKY FRIEDMAN

*

God Bless John Wayne

faber and faber

LONDON · BOSTON

Australian edition first published in 1995
by Faber and Faber Limited
3 Queen Square, London WC1N 3AU
Open market paperback edition first published in 1995
UK paperback edition first published in 1996
This paperback edition first published in 1997

Phototypeset by Intype London Ltd
Printed and bound in Great Britain by
Mackays of Chatham PLC, Chatham, Kent

A CIP record for this book is
available from the British Library

ISBN 0–571–17947–9

To my kid sister Marcie

'And to tell you the truth this telephone booth gets
    lonesome in the rain,
But, son, I'm 23 in Nashville and I'm 47 in Maine.
And when your mama gets home would you tell
    her I phoned – it'd take a lifetime to explain
That I'm a country picker with a bumpersticker that
    says: God Bless John Wayne.'

From 'People Who Read People Magazine'
by Kinky Friedman

ONE
*

It was raining cool cats and kosher hot dogs in the city that afternoon and things weren't getting any sunnier as the cat looked over my shoulder at me looking over my bank statement. I was keeping us in cigars and tuna by tackling a murder investigation every now and then, but the big clients didn't seem to be queuing up on the street outside my building waiting for me to throw down the little black puppet head with the key to the front door wedged in its mouth.

In fact, things were so bad that the only person who'd sought my help recently in undertaking an investigation for him had been Ratso. Ratso was my flamboyant flea market friend who sometimes served as a rather weather-beaten Dr Watson to my postnasal Sherlock Holmes. In his role of Dr Watson he brought zero sophistication to the table – any table – but he was loyal to a fault, was possessed of a rather charming naïveté, and had a good heart, which any detective worth his low-sodium salt will tell you is invariably the greatest possible obstacle to understanding the criminal mind.

Ratso as Dr Watson I could deal with. Ratso as a client was a whole other animal, and I do mean animal. So, when Ratso first mentioned the matter to me, I demurred. About the fourth time he mentioned it, I inquired as to the nature of the investigation, and he'd said, 'Well, it's really a very personal matter,' and I'd suggested, perhaps a bit unkindly, 'then why don't you keep it to yourself?' The other bad thing about having Ratso as a client was that he'd never paid for a meal or picked up a check in his life and there was every reason to believe that working for him would very definitely not be a financial pleasure.

I was seriously thinking of hanging myself from the shower

rod when the phones rang. I maintain two red telephones on my desk, each exactly an arm's length to the east and the west of the tip of my cigar. They are both attached to the same line and when they ring in tandem things can get pretty exciting around the loft.

In this particular instance, the cat leapt up onto the desk, knocking my large, Texas-shaped ashtray upside down onto my crotch. The concept of my crotch shaped like the state of Texas was something I could've probably lived with if it weren't for so many tourists gawking. I removed the ashtray and picked up the blower on the left.

'Start talkin',' I said.

'Sergeant Mort Cooperman referred us to you,' said a well-cultivated woman's voice. 'He's told us all about you.'

'Well,' I said, 'I hope it was all good.'

There was a silence on the line that lasted, I thought, a little longer than necessary. I relit a fairly ancient cigar and waited patiently.

'I'm calling on behalf of a gentleman of such prominence and the matter in question is one of such sensitivity that we could hardly turn it over to the police or any large investigative agency. The story would be headlines in all the tabloids. I cannot overemphasize the importance of discretion and decorum in this matter. That's why we settled on calling you.'

'Get off the goddamn desk,' I said to the cat in a stage whisper.

'I beg your pardon?'

'Nothing,' I said. 'Domestic problem.'

'There will, of course,' she continued, 'be a very handsome retainer.'

'My teeth are fine,' I said. 'God's my orthodontist.'

There was a fairly long silence on the line. The woman, obviously, was not amused. I looked up at the cat and saw that the cat, obviously, was not amused either. If you always spent

2

your time trying to entertain women and cats, I reflected, life could be a hard room to work.

'He would like to meet you today,' the woman continued, 'at two o'clock at Le Cirque.'

'Korean place?' I said.

'Hardly,' said the woman.

She gave me the address of the restaurant and I jotted it down in my Big Chief Tablet. The cat watched the paper as I wrote and then gave a rather bored feline shrug.

'Just mention your name to the maître d',' said the woman, 'and he'll show you to the private table.'

'Hold the weddin',' I said. 'I'm not going out in the freezing cold and rain to some fancy frog restaurant and mention my name to some quivering-nostriled maître d' without knowing the party that is of such prominence that you can't even tell me his name over the phone.'

There was a pause. Then there was the sound of an Aryan sigh. I puffed on the cigar and waited for the blower to emit further information into my left earlobe. When the woman spoke again it was to say only one word, her tone and inflection like the low, painful murmuring of a whore in confessional.

'Rockefeller,' she said, and hung up.

I cradled the blower, sat back in my chair, and puffed thoughtfully on the cigar.

'Where have I heard that name?' I said to the cat.

TWO
*

I put my feet up on the desk, puffed pridefully on the cigar, and thought it over for a few moments. That's the way the really big

3

cases happened these days, I figured. A beautiful woman in black doesn't walk into your office anymore. Instead, you get an invitation to do lunch at Le Cirque. It troubled me slightly that I hadn't even bothered to find out my potential client's first name. Of course, if your last name is Rockefeller, I reasoned, you don't really need a first name.

At one-thirty I put on my cowboy hat, heavy coat, and no-hunting vest with cigars in the little stitched ammunition loops, and walked out the door of the loft.

I left the cat in charge.

I stepped into the freight elevator, which boasted one exposed lightbulb and all the ambience of a movable meat locker, and drifted down to the little lobby like a lost snowflake. If some scion of the Rockefeller family had gotten his tail in a crack, why would Sergeant Cooperman put them in touch with me? On the other hand, I might be the perfect choice if you wished to eschew all trappings of the establishment. And, though I was still in the beginner's-luck department, I did have a fairly impressive little string of crime-solving successes going for me. Cooperman, of all people, would be keenly aware of that.

I walked out onto Vandam Street and the cold rain cut through me like a drag queen with a bowie knife. The leftover slush on the sidewalk from yesterday's snow was the color of coffee and about four inches deep. It was a hell of a day to be having lunch with a Rockefeller. It was also a hell of a day to be looking for a cab. It was so cold I was ready to jump aboard any yellow four-wheeled penis with a sign on top, even if the only Rockefeller I'd ever really wanted to meet was Michael and the odds of that happening this side of the ozone layer were six-to-five against.

There were no cabs. Cabs, apparently, thought I was dead. So I ankled it through the slush in my brontosaurus foreskin cowboy boots and I counted maître d's to keep my brain stem at least active enough not to turn into a toxic icicle. I didn't like

4

maître d's much, I reflected, and to be fair I must report that most maître d's I'd encountered didn't like me much either. I did not have what you might call a Judy Garland-like rapport with that distinctly Cerberean species. Nobody really liked maître d's at these coochi-poochi-boomalini frog places anyway, I figured. They were effete, power-hungry, phony, officious little boogers for the most part. Not even the most misunderstood child in Belgium wanted to grow up to be a maître d'. About the only charitable thing you could say about them was they were good diversionary subject matter to think about when you were freezing your Swedish meatballs off.

I hooked a left at the corner and trudged up Hudson thinking about the possibility of representing a Rockefeller on my next case. Not too shabby. The nature of the case almost didn't matter as long as I somehow managed to blither my way to a successful solution. The referrals that could flow out of something like that might really be top drawer. The prestige that would accrue to me would be almost unimaginable. I might even be able to make a living.

Of course, if I took the Rockefeller case, discretion and even secrecy would probably have to come with the territory. It would have to be a solo gig. I'd have to keep the Village Irregulars, who'd been invaluable in the past, away with a barge pole. Ratso, of course; McGovern, my large Irish legman; Rambam, the investigator who'd spent time in federal never-never land; all would have to be kept entirely in the dark. Likewise, I'd have to distance myself professionally from Mick Brennan, Pete Myers, Chinga Chavin, and Cleve, who was the easiest of all to distance myself from. He was currently residing in the Pilgrim State Mental Hospital for smoking country singers a few years back at the Lone Star Café. There were, fortunately, no plans to release Cleve anytime soon. If that fateful day ever did come, however, the only smart thing for the rest of the world to do would be to immediately check itself into the Pilgrim State Mental Hospital.

There were very few people on the street and those who were there looked like outpatients themselves. They were on the street because there was no other place for them to go and if there had been, the maître d' probably wouldn't have let them in. They all looked cold, desperate, lonely, with maybe a sidecar of criminally insane. I was glad I didn't have a rearview mirror attached to my forehead. I might've gotten a glimpse of myself.

After about ten blocks of tertiary tedium, I vaulted into a cab that appeared to be driven by the President of Lesotho, and we spun our way across the glittering, shivering web of side streets and avenues until we pulled up in front of the promised land, Le Cirque.

'Can I help you?' said the maître d', as he studied my cowboy hat. The phrase can mean almost anything in New York, depending on how it's said and who's talking down to whom.

I mentioned my name.

His nostrils quivered ever so slightly. I was very gratified.

'Right this way, Mr Friedman,' he said. I followed him through a strange city of mostly oblivious diners bent upon eating their escargots, which was fine with me. If you're not bent upon eating your escargots, your escargots will fall into your lap and leave greasy, iridescent, possibly radioactive dead snail trails that quite conceivably have a half-life of about twenty thousand years and could cause problems later down the line at the dry cleaners. It's just the snail's way of saying to the people: 'Piss off, mate.'

I followed the back of the man's head for a long time. I didn't care if he was leading me to the gates of hell or a table too close to the kitchen; at least it was warm. When you walk past people who are busy eating, you see them but they only half-see you. You'll draw a few odd looks, maybe an occasional moue of distaste. Somebody'll start a friendly smile but then think better of it; somebody'll stare at you like you're a cockroach. But most of the people will care less. And then you're gone. It's a lot like life.

The maître d' very deferentially waved me to my private table. The only thing private about it was that there was nobody else there.

'Your guest will be arriving shortly, sir,' said the maître d'.

'Guest?' I said to the man's buttocks as he walked away. '*I'm* the goddamned guest.'

I sat for a while and listened to the subtle, slightly obscene sounds of the clanking of silverware. It all seemed somehow connected – the people, the plates, the forks and knives and spoons – like one large piece of ridiculous machinery that feeds itself forever, occasionally giving out with a subdued belch over here and a high-pitched, polite little Brenda Lee-type fart over there, and quite frequently, gushing forth with the ugly sounds of rich people's laughter.

I stared at a chandelier for a while, then caught a waiter's eye and ordered a double shot of Jameson. To pass the time waiting for my drink I contented myself with making eye contact with a child at a nearby table. The kid seemed genuinely interested in my outfit and my cigar, which, out of courtesy to my fellow diners remained, for the moment, unlit.

'Ever seen a real cowboy before?' I said to the kid.

The kid's mother, whose head resembled that of a pet ferret with earrings, gave me an icy stare and then turned her withering visage on the child.

'Guess not,' I said.

By the time my second double Jameson had arrived I'd enjoyed about all the marvelous ambience I could stand and was considering lighting a cigar just to see if anybody was awake. They say if you light a cigarette the waiter immediately shows up with your food. But if you really want some action, try lighting a cigar in a restaurant. People begin oohing and aahhing and murmuring like a German forest, or coughing that dry practiced, controlled little California cough that makes you want to throttle them. Then they begin rushing hither and thither, calling 911, wagging their fingers, feigning nausea,

7

and frenetically jumping through their assholes to show they care. If Elijah walked in right then he'd never get a table. Everybody in the place would be too clinically focused on a man smoking a cigar, and of course, Elijah couldn't sit with me. I was waiting for Rockefeller.

As it turned out, I didn't have long to wait.

I'd just killed most of my second round and was giving some serious thought to visiting the little private investigators' room, when the maître d' began walking briskly toward my private table. There was a half-obscured figure moving along right behind him in the fashionably dim aquarium lighting. Something about the second figure seemed to set off a rather jangly car alarm on a backstreet somewhere in my gray matter department.

Then, suddenly, as if in a dream, the maître d' was handing me a menu, stepping quickly aside, and immediately vanishing, as did any remaining hope I'd had of experiencing a pleasant, productive afternoon. The man sitting across from me now was wearing a coonskin cap with the animal's little head still attached to the front, eyes sewn shut. He was also wearing green pants and an especially repellent lox-colored sport coat. He was giggling to himself in a loud and rather unpleasant manner.

My anger mounted steadily as he sat across the table pretending to coolly peruse his menu while fighting to control his somewhat obvious prepubescent glee. Finally, it seemed, he could contain himself no longer.

'Allow me to introduce myself,' he said. 'I'm Ratso Rockefeller.'

THREE

*

Two mornings later, still slightly smarting from the Ratso Rockefeller scam, as well as getting hosed by Ratso into paying the check, I was loitering around the loft in my purple bathrobe, sipping an espresso and spending a little quality time with the cat.

'One of the truly irritating aspects of knowing Ratso,' I said to the cat, 'is that no matter how repellent his behavior, you can't stay angry at him long. That quality alone is enough to piss me off.'

The cat had never liked Ratso. Being of a far more unforgiving and intransigent nature than myself, the cat had consistently disliked Ratso for inexplicable reasons, going all the way back to the time when Ratso was a housepest at the loft and the cat had taken a Nixon in his red antique shoe, which had once belonged to a dead man. Technically, I suppose, the shoe could never actually have *belonged* to a dead man. It was just that Ratso, as a matter of custom, obtained his entire wardrobe from flea markets and back alleyways and seemed to derive an inordinate amount of pride from the fact that the previous owners of his apparel had gone to Jesus.

'How could you sustain a grudge against a guy like that?' I said to the cat.

The cat focused nine lifetimes of green-eyed feline malevolence directly through my left iris into whatever remained inside my cranium.

'I see,' I said.

I paced the loft for a few minutes. Then I came back again to the cat.

'Ratso told me something shockingly personal the other day

9

at a very coochi-poochi-boomalini restaurant,' I said. 'He needs my help.'

But now the cat was asleep.

I was just lighting my first cigar of the morning, taking some little care to keep the tip of the cigar ever so slightly above the flame from the kitchen match, when I heard what sounded like a large, somewhat agitated pelican shrieking outside my window. My window was on the fourth floor of the old refurbished warehouse, and through the grime I could plainly see that no pelican or stork of any kind was resting on my windowsill. The only thing on the windowsill was a fairly sizable quantity of residual pigeon shit of a fashionably off-white color and shaped strikingly like a map of the later Hapsburg Empire.

This raised two distinct possibilities. Either my hearing had gone through some uncanny enhancement process recently or the pelican was a ventriloquist. As I turned the matter over in my mind, the invisible pelican shrieked again, this time much louder. Also, quite amazingly, it appeared to be calling my name.

Against my better judgment, I walked over to the window again and flung it open. A frigid tail wind blew into the loft, sending the cockroaches scurrying. The cat sat on the desk, watching me with a critical eye. She did not suffer fools gladly. In fact she did not suffer anyone gladly and this is something I'd spoken to her about on a number of occasions, usually after I'd had three or four shots of Jameson.

I stuck my head out the window and immediately felt my nose hairs turn to stalactites. I looked down and saw a large figure pacing back and forth rapidly on the frozen sidewalk below. It was Rambam.

'Throw down that fuckin' puppet head,' he shouted.

I removed the little black puppet head from the top of the refrigerator. It had a bright parachute attached, the key to the building in its mouth, and a big smile on its face, which is more than you could say for most people in New York. I tossed the puppet head out and watched it sail gracefully down into Rambam's iron grip. Then I slammed down the window and poured myself another cup of steaming espresso.

Moments later Rambam and I were sitting at the kitchen table, sipping espresso and looking at each other from opposite sides of my old chessboard. The set was rather dusty, little used these days, and at the moment featured a long, ambitious cobweb stretching all the way from the white queen to the black knight at king's bishop three.

'This is the chess set,' I said, 'that I once used to play the world grand master Samuel Reshevsky. He came to Houston, played fifty people simultaneously, beat us all. I was the youngest player. I was only seven years old at the time. Can you imagine that? Seven years old.'

I puffed on the cigar and contemplated the old board. Rambam sipped his espresso.

'What have you done for us lately?' he said.

'Well, I'm getting ready to try to help Ratso,' I said. 'He's got a little problem.'

'He certainly does,' said Rambam.

'Ratso told me something in confidence the other night,' I said, glossing over the Rockefeller ruse so as not to get Rambam distracted.

'Whatever it is,' said Rambam, 'I don't want to know.' There was no particular love lost amongst some of the Village Irregulars.

'The only reason I'm telling you is so *you* can help *me* help Ratso.'

'Why should I help Ratso?' said Rambam. 'He wouldn't piss on me if I was on fire.'

'That *is* asking a lot,' I said.

'Look. I'm working on a lot of shit right now. Just tell me what his problem is and I'll tell you how I would go about taking care of it if the problem belonged to anyone else in the world but Ratso. Then you just do what I would've done and everything'll be fine.'

'Then I'll be a real grown-up private investigator?' I said.

'No,' said Rambam. 'You'll be an idiot for helping Ratso.'

If the truth be known, I was already smiling a little bit when I thought of the unlikely countenance of Ratso Rockefeller. Besides, everything is funny if you wait long enough. This time it'd only taken me two days. For some humorless, constipated people it takes a lifetime for them to see that their mere existence is a joke and even then sometimes they don't get it.

'Ratso said that almost no one knows this about him – '

'Almost no one cares,' said Rambam.

' – but he was adopted. He was always told that his real mother died in childbirth but some new evidence has turned up to indicate she might still be alive. No one knows who the father was. He wants me to help him find his true birth parents.'

Rambam did not look excited. He got up, walked over to the espresso machine, and made himself another espresso. Then he stood by the kitchen counter and patted the cat. The cat was just perverse enough to tolerate Rambam. I, unfortunately, was just perverse enough to tolerate Ratso.

'I'll tell you what I'll do,' said Rambam finally. 'You find out the name of Ratso's birth mother and I'll help you find her wherever she's currently living, which, having observed Ratso's table manners on a number of occasions, is probably East Roratunga.'

'Thanks, Rambam,' I said. 'That's very Christian of you for an outspoken, militant Hebe.'

Rambam, however, wasn't listening. He was stroking the cat and staring out the window, shaking his head ever so slightly. There was a dangerous little smile on his face.

'That bastard,' he said.

'That's clever,' I said, 'but it's also a bit cold.'

'C'mon,' said Rambam. 'Would you ever want to adopt a little orphan Ratso?'

'Of course not,' I said, turning dramatically toward the cat to enlarge my audience. There seemed to be just a hint of disapproval in the cat's eyes.

'But I have always wanted,' I continued hurriedly, 'to adopt an adult Korean.'

FOUR
*

'I've looked after a lot of lost sheep in my life,' said Ratso, later that evening as we walked through the colorful, jangly streets of Little Italy. The weather had warmed up a bit and was now what New Yorkers are fond of calling 'brisk'. Anywhere else they'd call it cold as hell.

'Now,' said Ratso, as he gazed at a young family through a restaurant window, 'I find I am one.'

The notion of Ratso as a lost sheep, for some reason, saddened me. He was, no doubt, a lot of things, most of them unpleasant. But some vestige of a still, small voice within me did not want my friend to see himself in such a pathetic light. The voice said: 'Help him, but don't ever count on getting paid.'

'You're not a lost sheep,' I said. 'Just because you've fallen in love with a succession of girlfriends all of whom happen to have about forty-nine broken wings –'

'My dick isn't a psychiatrist,' said Ratso.

'If it was,' I said, 'I never would've slept on your couch.'

I thought, a bit ruefully, of the many times I'd availed myself of Ratso's couch, before I had a cat, or a loft, or anything faintly

13

resembling a job. Back when I was a lost sheep myself. Now that I'd grown up to become an adult stamp collector, it was my turn to help Ratso. I vowed to myself that I wouldn't let him down.

'It's a funny thing,' he said, as we sat across from each other at one of the little tables in Luna's Restaurant, 'but finding out that my mother is a real person with a real identity who may still be alive has been very unsettling to me. My whole life I was led to believe she died when I was born.'

'Who told you that?'

'My dad,' said Ratso.

I thought of Ratso's dad – his adoptive father – Jack Sloman, who'd died quite recently in Florida. I'd met him a few times. He was a kind man. Very proud of his son.

'I went to Florida several times to see my father before he died,' said Ratso. 'But with the stroke and Alzheimer's he was too far gone to talk. He recognized me and seemed almost to understand what I was saying, but all he could do was lie there and make noises like a little bird.'

All of us would probably make noises like a little bird some day, I thought. If we were lucky. The waiter brought our orders of linguini with red clam sauce and in addition, for Ratso, a huge cauldron of zuppa di pesce. He attacked the food like a frenzied priest going after an altar boy.

'At least your troubles don't seem to be affecting your appetite,' I said.

'I'm a lost sheep,' said Ratso. 'Not an anorexic sheep.'

'So what makes you think your real mother may still be alive?'

'My mother mentioned it last week. She's in a retirement community in Florida – '

'That's my dream,' I said. 'To be one of the Shalom Retirement Village People. Maybe your mother and I will put together a band.'

'You tried that once,' said Ratso. 'Anyway, she alluded to

some new information about my real mother that my dad had kept in a safe deposit box. She said he wanted me to have it opened after he died.'

'Jesus,' I said. 'Where's the safe deposit box?'

'In a bank.'

'I know it's in a bank, Ratso. With my vast experience in the field of crime solving, I was able to deduce that. Where's the goddamn bank?'

'Florida.'

'So just have your mother go to the bank, open the safe deposit box, and send what's ever in there to you.'

Ratso extracted the tentacles of a squid from the zuppa di pesce, put it in his mouth, and shook his head, apparently in answer to my suggestion.

'I don't want to do that,' he said. 'She's upset enough about everything already and it wouldn't be right for me to go on some active, personal crusade to find my birth parents right now. That's how I want you to help me. Go down to Florida. Talk to my mother. Talk to the bank. Get into the safe deposit box. I don't want to talk to my mother about my true birth mother just now. I don't know if I ever want to involve her in this. She is the only mother I've ever known and I don't want to hurt her. Also, I'm somewhat ambivalent myself at times about finding my real mother.'

'And I'm somewhat ambivalent about getting on a plane and going down to Florida and not knowing who's paying for it.'

'No problem,' said Ratso. 'Just put it on my tab.'

Later, as we trudged along the Italian ice of Mulberry Street, Ratso's mood seemed, if possible, to deepen. But, like all his outlandish outfits and dead men's accoutrements, he wore his self-pity well. I knew I had to help him find some answers. Either that or coddle a large Jewish meatball for the rest of my natural life.

'I appreciate your helping me,' Ratso said, as we rounded a

corner and headed toward a small café he favored because they had about a thousand different kinds of cannolis.

'I haven't said I'll help yet.'

'You will.'

'I couldn't chance losing my Dr Watson. You bring such a charming naïveté to a case.'

'Especially this one,' he said grimly. He stopped under a street lamp and removed from his wallet a small, ancient-looking piece of paper.

'What's that?' I said. 'A leftover bar mitzvah card?'

'It's older than that, if you can believe it. It's the card for the lawyer who arranged my adoption.'

'Surely he's woken up in hell by now.'

'Probably. I think he was a pretty shady guy. I can't tell you how many times in the past I've thought about trying to find him, but something kept stopping me. It's like I wanted to know but I didn't want to know – now it's probably too late.'

'Well, make up your rabbit mind. I'm not going to work my balls off digging up this information and then call your ass and find out you don't want to know.'

'I want to know. I just don't want to find out on my own.' He handed me the lawyer's card.

'If I find out the truth,' I said, putting the old business card in my pocket, 'I'm going to tell you. I'm not going to hold anything back.'

'Even if it's her?' said Ratso, as he gazed across the brightly lit street, an infinite sadness in his eyes.

I followed his gaze to a squalid figure standing on the curbside beneath a window display of Mussolini T-shirts. Somehow she appeared more like an ephemeral shadow than a human being. A disreputable shawl or blanket covered her head and most of her body and what apparently were her worldly possessions resided in two large plastic garbage bags even now spilling over into the gutter. She looked for all the world like some half-forgotten character out of a Dickens novel, and when

16

her eyes met mine very briefly they seemed like fireflies disappearing into the primeval night.

'Even if it's her,' I said.

We walked a little further and I lit a cigar. I was puffing on it thoughtfully as the café came into sight.

'Let's get one thing straight,' I said. 'I'm not going to investigate this because I feel sorry for you. You're *not* a lost sheep.'

I looked at Ratso carefully. In the neon incandescence of Little Italy his face reflected all the pain of a momentary mask of Greek tragedy.

'Okay, Sherlock,' he said. 'So I'm *not* a lost sheep. Then what the hell *am* I?'

I glanced briefly at the happy people sitting inside the little café. I puffed on the cigar and watched the smoke curl up past the street lamp and vanish in the lights of the city.

'You're a fucked-up shepherd,' I said.

FIVE
*

As the late-morning sun filtered feebly into the loft, the cat sat on my desk and studied the lawyer's business card. I leaned back in my chair, leisurely sipping an espresso and smoking a cigar. If the guy had handled Ratso's adoption proceedings, by my reckoning he was almost certainly worm bait by now. Either that, or his scattered ashes were doing their dead-level best to perpetuate the city's pollution problems.

'Have I missed something?' I said to the cat.

The cat said nothing. She continued her rather intense perusal of the small document.

'Guy's got to be in some vacant lot in Brooklyn,' I said. 'Probably pushing up poison ivy.'

The cat stared at the card. I puffed patiently on the cigar.

'You know, the life span of most lawyers is often briefer than their briefs. They're very anal retentive, they make a lot of money usually, and quite often in order to do that they wind up screwing a lot of people and God punishes them. Of course, as the poet Kenneth Patchen once said: "Nobody's a long time." That includes amateur detectives and cats. Especially cats who stare too long at business cards.'

I got up to pour another espresso from the large silver-and-bronze commercial-size espresso machine. The machine was sent to me several years back by a nice gentleman named Joe the Hyena, whom I've never met and with any luck never will. Why he sent it and where it might've come from is a laborious and, I suspect, rather unsavory story which falls into the some-things-are-better-not-to-know department.

I poured the espresso and was returning to the desk when a dull thudding sound began to emanate downward from the ceiling of the loft. Winnie Katz's lesbian dance class was at it again, and what exactly went on up there was another thing that I didn't really want to know. The cat looked up at the ceiling with an irritated expression, switched her tail back and forth a few times rather viciously, then resumed her vigil over the card.

'Maybe you've got something there,' I said to the cat. 'Pardon my boardinghouse reach.'

I picked up the card and studied it again, this time with a softer focus. After all, I reflected, this worn old business card, this artifact, was all Ratso had to hold on to. It'd been in his possession since he was a young boy, he'd said. It was all that was left of a mother and father he could only dream about. The mere taking of the card from Ratso, I now realized, was practically tantamount to a spiritual commitment on my part.

The lawyer's name was William Hamburger, a slightly

humorous and unusual name, and that was good. Even in New York there couldn't be that many guys named Hamburger.

The firm was Hamburger & Hamburger. It was one of those firms, I briefly explained to the cat, where you could call up and say: 'Is Mr Hamburger in?' and they'd say, 'No, he's away from the office', and you could say 'Well, then, is Mr Hamburger in?' Unfortunately, the address and phone number did not look particularly humorous or promising. It was an address in Brooklyn on Court Street and the phone number was preceded by the letters 'UL', which might've stood for 'Ulster', but in this case, more appropriately could've stood for 'Ulcer', because trying to run down something this old very likely was going to give me one.

'Where there's a will, there's a lawyer,' I said to the cat. 'Let's call him.'

I dialed the number.

'Hel-lo,' said a man with an oriental accent thick enough to float wontons on. If this was William Hamburger, he must have been to Buddha and back a few times by now.

'Good morning, sir,' I said in an important voice. 'I'm trying to locate a Mr William Hamburger.'

'No have hamburger,' said the man.

'Hold the weddin',' I said. 'I don't want to *eat* hamburger – I want to *find* him. He's a lawyer who had this phone number years ago.'

'Awwwww,' said the man. 'You mean *royer*. He die many years ago. But son take over business. Move to rower Manhattan. Son big royer now.'

'Son big royer now,' I said to the cat after I'd hung up with the guy. The cat was curled up under the desk lamp and showed no reaction whatsoever. This did not surprise me, since she had demonstrated no sense of humor either, from the time I'd first known her. She did deign to open her eyes halfway and stare at me with a very thinly veiled moue of distaste. Or maybe it was a mew of distaste. This wasn't terribly surprising

19

either, for cats are very politically correct creatures. Ethnic mimicry sends them up the wall.

I lit a fresh cigar, picked up the blower on the left, and dialed Manhattan information.

'What city?' said a bored male voice with a high-octane lisp.

'Manhattan.'

'How can I help you?' he said, in a voice that made it clear he wouldn't throw a rubber swan to a drowning man.

'How many Hamburgers you got in Manhattan?'

'Twelve billion served,' he said, really going to town on the word 'served.'

'Let me rephrase that,' I said. 'How many *people* named Hamburger you got?'

'Let me see,' he said.

I waited. He hummed. The cat slept. The investigation was not exactly roaring off the starting line. But I'd expected this. Rambam had told me that most searches for birth parents can be tedious, futile, and quite often, stultifyingly dull. So far, he wasn't wrong.

By the time the operator had finished counting Hamburgers, I was beginning preparations to hang myself by the heels from the bronze eagle on the top of the espresso machine. Finally, he stopped humming and spoke again.

'About ten,' he said.

'And how many live in lower Manhattan?'

The operator sighed a very audible, theatrical sigh. But he did resume his humming. I took this as an encouraging sign.

'Three,' he said, somewhat peevishly.

'Great,' I said. 'Can you give me those three numbers?'

He sighed again, but this time he didn't really seem to have his heart in it. Eventually, if somewhat coyly, he coughed up the information.

'Thanks,' I said. 'Sorry these weren't the kind of hamburgers you eat.'

'How can you be so sure?' he said.

I began calling the lower Manhattan Hamburgers and nailed the lawyer the first time out of the box. Things were picking up.

By stating that the matter was one of great urgency I was able to get an appointment with the lawyer – whose name was Moie Hamburger – that very afternoon. Of course, 'urgent' was not quite the proper word to apply to this investigation. The case was already older than God. Also, my client wasn't sure that he wanted to know the results. But these days New York has become so crazy that things have to be urgent. Important doesn't work anymore.

Before I left for my meeting with Moie Hamburger, I called Rambam to make sure I knew what I was looking for. Rambam said that having the lawyer run a file check would be the easiest but the guy might charge me my eldest son for the fee. I told Rambam I didn't have an eldest son. 'How can you be so sure?' he said. I told him that was the second time I'd been asked that question and I never wanted anyone to ask me that again. 'How can you be so sure?' he said.

According to Rambam, if I didn't want to spring for the file check, I'd have to check the files myself, with the lawyer's permission, of course. Rambam guessed they'd probably be in some old warehouse in Brooklyn, the thought of which caused me to roll my eyeballs toward the lesbian dance class. Again, according to Rambam, I was looking for legal files, case notes that pertained to applications for custody, or custody transfers. All actual court files, he said, would probably be sealed.

'Just like my fate is sealed,' I said.

'He's *your* friend,' said Rambam cheerfully, as he hung up the phone.

A short time later, I grabbed a handful of cigars along with my hat and coat, killed all the lights except for the cat's heat lamp on the desk, and headed for the door.

'I'm off to see the *royer*,' I said.

She didn't even flinch.

SIX
*

Unless you're planning on making a pilgrimage to the grave of Clarence Darrow, a visit to an attorney rarely manifests itself as a particularly spiritual experience. Folks who come to lawyers usually have a problem. By the time they leave the lawyer's office they usually have a complicated, expensive problem. Lawyers don't intentionally try to make things costlier or more tedious for their clients. They just can't help themselves. It is the way of their people.

Moie Hamburger, of the lower Manhattan Hamburgers, I suspected, was no exception. The outer office of the firm was all done up in about eleven shades of tasteful, decorous, extremely expensive-looking gray. Not only would a file check be fiscally out of the question here, you'd probably have to leave a retainer the size of the battleship *Potemkin* if you wanted them to check your hat.

I gave my name to the receptionist and she gave me a surprisingly ingenuous smile. Probably new in town. I sat down on a couch the color of twilight, picked up a *Wall Street Gerbil*, and watched as the busy little secretaries and paralegal types rushed hither and thither carrying thick sheaves of important-looking documents, all very likely generated by somebody's highly insured four-wheeled penis allegedly being tail-ended by a Dodge Dart or by some alert individual allegedly getting himself photographed down at the No-Tell Motel in the explicit act of coveting his neighbor's ass. Needless to say, everything was now safely in the hands of the lawyers.

Allegedly.

Moie Hamburger's office, I soon discovered, was comprised of still more shades of gray, including Hamburger himself, who was a bit more o-l-d than I'd expected. I lamped him for being

22

in his late sixties, meaning he'd conceivably still have been in law school at the time his father first became fatefully entangled with the spiritual tar baby that the world now knew as Larry 'Ratso' Sloman.

Hamburger was a distinguished-looking, kindly-visaged man with a big white beard that, unlike the rhetoric of most lawyers, came to a point. Hundreds of years ago in Norway or someplace he would've made a good-looking king. More evidence for my theory that all of us are drawn to occupations for which we're horribly ill suited. Unfortunately, the theory also applied to me.

As I entered the narrow entranceway to the office, a large, hirsute individual who roughly resembled an abominable snowman with a chip on his shoulder, barreled by me on the left. I did a little, quickly improvised Texas two-step out of his way and walked over to Hamburger's large, well-polished, important-looking desk.

'What was that?' I said, nodding in the direction of the empty passageway.

'Just a client,' said Hamburger with a rueful smile, 'who's been with the firm a long time.'

'In that case,' I said, 'I'll just be a moment.'

'How can I help you, Mr Friedman?' he said, beginning to show a few signs of mild irritation.

'Why don't we start with this,' I said, as I placed the archaic business card on his desk.

'Wow,' said Hamburger, as he looked at the card. His face appeared to soften with a brief spasm of something like nostalgia, then, just as quickly, became a mask of some more contemporary countenance, possibly wariness or distrust, which almost caused him to squirm. 'How'd you come into possession of this?' he said.

'A friend gave it to me,' I said. 'I figured the way to the father was through the son.'

'That path may prove a little difficult,' said Hamburger. 'My father died twenty years ago.'

'Sorry to hear that,' I said.

'So I ask you again,' he said, with a few more slight stirrings of irritation, 'how can I help you, Mr Friedman?' The card was still on his desk but it had become again what it always had been, a thing of the past.

'My friend, the one who gave me your father's card, was adopted. Your father handled the adoption proceedings. My friend never knew his real parents. He was always led to believe his mother had died in childbirth. Now, with the death of his adoptive father, his mother has mentioned to him that there may be documents in a bank deposit box in Florida that say otherwise.'

'Have you checked these documents?' said Hamburger. There was a rather intense curiosity in his face.

'I shall,' I said. 'But first I'd like to get a little background here in New York. That would start with your old files.'

'What's your friend's name?' asked Hamburger.

'Larry Sloman,' I said. 'Known to his intimates as Ratso.' One blue vein was pulsating rather noticeably in Moie Hamburger's forehead.

'Running a formal file check on that period would be very expensive for you and not possible for us right now. What I can do is give you an authorization to our legal warehouse in Brooklyn. Just show it to the guard and go on up and sort through it yourself. Those old files, if they're still there, should be on the fifth floor, section fourteen. I'm not at all sure you'll find what you're looking for, but happy hunting.'

Hamburger drew a sheet of stationery with his firm's legal letterhead from his desk and proceeded to scribble a few sentences. He paused somewhat somberly and then signed his name, as if the document were of some grave import. I got up, he handed me the page, and I thanked him and headed for the door.

'There's something I think you ought to know,' he said. I stopped and turned around.

'Lay it on me,' I said.

'I'm not at liberty to give you any names or details,' said Hamburger, as looked into his suddenly rather chilly blue eyes. 'But you're not the first to approach me about this matter.'

SEVEN
*

Most people in Manhattan believe that if they travel outside of Manhattan proper the world is flat and they may very well fall off the map and end up in Brooklyn or Queens or worse. This is a highly evolved, extremely progressive idea, which has required generations of lasagna and pastrami sandwiches in order to fully develop. Certainly the trip was fraught with many dangers, not the least of which was that my cab driver bore a more than passing resemblance to Idi Amin. Eventually, we fell off the end of the map and ended up in front of a grim, forbidding-looking building somewhere in the bowels of Brooklyn.

I paid the cabbie, showed Hamburger's note to a large man wearing a small hat, and strode purposefully into the shadowy warehouse. The elevator to the fifth floor was a blood relative to the one in my building on Vandam Street, which, now that I thought about it, had once been a warehouse itself. It was too bad elevators only moved up and down and never got a chance to meet each other. The occupants of the elevators not only moved up and down, of course, but could also move horizontally across the board.

Section fourteen was not hard to find, and I quickly set about searching for S for Sloman. So far so good. File cabinets populated the warehouse floor, which was like a small city of its own and, par for the course, the S files were residing in the penthouse. I pulled a dusty Jacob's ladder out of the corner and climbed step by step closer to Ratso's past, which heretofore had been shrouded in mystery. I knew roughly what I was looking for: application for custody, custody transfer, case notes, etc. The warehouse was cold as hell but if the Angel of Death didn't push me off the ladder and I didn't break my neck, I felt I was getting warm.

I found the Sloman file, slipped it out of the cabinet, and navigated my way down the ladder, holding the file in my teeth and using my cigar as ballast. The Flying Wallenda Brothers come to Brooklyn. I walked over to a grime-covered window and opened the file.

I speed-read through the usual legal mumbo-jumbo until I got to the line where Ratso's mother's name was supposed to be. Either her name was 'Court File – Sealed' or I was going to have to look elsewhere for the truth. Ratso's adoptive parents, Jack and Lilyan, were there, surrounded by massive bookends of legal pronouncements. Ratso was born at Bellevue Hospital. He'd already told me that. Somewhere in all this ancient horse manure there had to be one live maggot.

Sure enough, on the last page of the file, under the heading 'Amended Petition' I found the only real news flash in the pile. No man is an island they say, unless that island happens to be called Manhattan. Or, as my friend Speed Vogel once put it rather succinctly: 'Your heart attack, my hangnail.' And yet I was mildly surprised at how a cold fact that was forty-seven years old and unknown even to Ratso had affected me. The statement in question read: 'No claim exists to minor child except that of mother; male parent now known to be deceased.'

At least there was one less person to look for.

EIGHT

*

By the time I got out of the warehouse, evening was falling
clumsily onto a cold, leaden landscape that appeared to have
been painted by some Van Gogh on his way to the corner liquor
store. That's where I was headed, too. There was a pay phone
on the corner and I wanted to call Ratso.

As I ankled down to the corner, the wind seemed to pick up
and the people appeared to scurry about like some new kind of
rodent. Newspapers full of yesterday's heroes swirled past me
along the sidewalk. I had all I could do to hold on to my
cowboy hat, so I didn't give a lot of thought to a man in a
black leather overcoat leaning against the side of the warehouse
shielding his face by trying to light a cigarette in the wind. I was
thinking about what I should tell Ratso.

When I got him on the phone I didn't tell him about his
father. I just made sure he'd be there and told him I was coming
by with an update on the investigation. I did this because,
though his father was a distant figure that he'd never known,
like a shadow on a wall in Hiroshima, his father was his father. I
also didn't say anything because another distant figure, the guy
in the black overcoat, had just gone inside the liquor store and
was now browsing the aisles, looking furtively in my direction.

I collared the blower and scanned the street for a hack for
hire. Nothing. When you need a hack in New York it's never
there, and when you don't they surround you like urine-
colored lava. Cabs are like women, or horses, or happiness, or
money, or pet parakeets. If you pursue them with great ardor
you'll never have them. If you honestly don't give a damn
they'll very often light right on your shoulder, in which case the
pet parakeet is, of course, preferable to the horse or the cab.

The guy in the liquor store picked up a bottle of something

that looked like Southern Comfort, held it for a moment, then put it back on the shelf. He had a good face to play cards with.

I thought back to Moie Hamburger's words as I'd left his office. 'You're not the first to approach me about this matter.' Terrific. All I needed was a *Day of the Jackal*-type character following me in Brooklyn. But why would anyone care? What was there about Ratso's misbegotten birth that would give a busy New Yorker pause?

I crossed the street and headed back up the block, and the guy came out of the liquor store and began following me like a baby duck imprinting its mother's tracks. I felt like a baby shmuck imprinting Ratso's mother's tracks. This guy was not a particularly invisible tail, but who would want me tailed in the first place? The obvious candidate was Moie Hamburger, but why would he bother to say, like a bride on her wedding night, 'You're not the first'? My paranoia was redlining.

After several blocks of hide-and-seek I finally spotted a large woman in a coat that must've decimated some mink's family tree, getting out of a cab and I took her place as the occupant. I left the guy in the black overcoat running down the sidewalk toward a parked car, gave the driver Ratso's address, and told him to step on it.

'Posse after you?' said the driver.

'I'll let you know,' I said.

I looked around a few times before we left Brooklyn. No posse. No cavalry. No Indians. No reason for anybody to give a damn whether or not I awkwardly stumbled toward the truth about the birth parents of one Larry 'Ratso' Sloman. No reason at all.

To play it safe, I jetted the cab a few blocks from Ratso's place on Prince Street in the Village. I loitered around an Italian bakery and a Korean greengrocer's store, but I saw no sign of the guy in the black overcoat. It had turned into a cold, dark night and I stepped into a corner grocery on Sullivan Street to get a large black coffee to go. I took a few sips and lit a cigar out on the sidewalk.

I'd never handled a missing-person case where you turned the clock back quite this far – almost fifty years. No doubt there were procedural methods and approaches to such an investigation but I didn't know what the hell they were. Rambam wasn't being overly helpful and I didn't know who else to turn to for advice. It was also possible, I thought darkly, that Ratso wasn't telling me everything. Maybe I wasn't asking him the right questions. I sipped some more coffee, took a few puffs on the cigar, and walked briskly up to his building, where I pushed 6G, which, according to Ratso, stood for God.

After an irritatingly long wait in the cold, I heard Ratso's rodent-like voice powering over the intercom.

'Who is it?' he said.

'It's the Antichrist,' I said, 'looking for 6G.'

'Come in, Antichrist,' he said.

I strolled quickly through the dingy, urine-scented foyer where Ratso's pet bum usually slept, took the elevator up to six, and leaned on Ratso's doorbell.

'Who is it?' shouted Ratso.

'Jesus Christ! Let me in!'

'Is it *Jesus* Christ or the *Antichrist*?' said Ratso. 'Please be specific. It could be important.'

'Please, Ratso. I've got to talk to you.' I also had to urinate like a racehorse.

'Sounds like Jesus Christ.'

'Goddamnit, Ratso, I'm gonna kill you.'

'Nope. It's the Antichrist.'

Eventually, I heard the various chains and bars and tumblers moving through their machinations as Ratso began the rather laborious process of opening his triple-locked door. What in the hell he was striving so zealously to protect was another question. How in the hell I'd gotten myself involved in this investigation was still another.

At last the door swung open and there was Ratso dressed in a coonskin cap, longjohn pajamas that looked like they'd once gone West with Lewis and Clark, and a pair of red shoes that I knew from past encounters had once belonged to a dead man.

'Kinkstah!' shouted Ratso enthusiastically. 'Why didn't you say it was you?'

'I'm going for a low profile on this case,' I said, as I endeavored to carefully navigate the narrow strait between Ratso's body and several hundred hockey sticks he kept precariously balanced against his doorframe.

'What've you got?' Ratso asked eagerly.

'I've got a full bladder, Ratso,' I said. 'Now if you'll get out of my way, I'd like to shake hands with the devil.'

'You *are* the Antichrist,' I heard Ratso say as I closed the door to his overheated bathroom, which was about the size of my nose.

Moments later I was pacing back and forth in Ratso's cluttered living room with Ratso comfortably ensconced on his famous couch with the skid marks on it. I'd once called that couch and this ragged, jumbled living room home. As I glanced around at the statue of the Virgin Mary, the polar bear's head, the ten thousand books on Jesus, Hitler, and Bob Dylan, the photos of Ratso shaking hands with Richard Nixon and posing with Bob Dylan (nothing with him and Jesus or Hitler, unfortunately), the two huge television screens soundlessly, simultaneously emitting a hockey game and a porno movie, I felt comforted with the knowledge that you can't go home again.

'Your real father is dead, Ratso,' I said softly. 'According to the application for custody that I found in the legal files.'

Ratso's form on the couch seemed suddenly forsaken. He watched the screens sightlessly and seemed to almost huddle there withdrawing ever so slightly into himself.

'What about my mother?' he said.

'Her name is not filled in on the appropriate line. Instead, it

30

reads: Court File – Sealed. I can check the records at Bellevue Hospital, but it's been a long time and it's a long shot. I may very well have to go to Florida before this is over.'

'You're a real friend, Kinkstah,' said Ratso. He picked up the remote control unit and killed the porno movie. 'I want you to find my mother,' he said.

A short time later, I'd put my coat on and lit up a fresh cigar, in preparation for departure. Ratso still remained where he was on the couch, silently following the silent hockey players while other thoughts, I knew, weaved back and forth across the far ice of his memory.

As I walked past an overpopulated coffee table on the way to the door I noticed a bill lying on top of a disorderly stack of books. It was from one Robert McLane, Private Investigator. The bill contended that Ratso was past due in paying him four hundred dollars for services rendered.

'What the hell is this?' I said, picking the bill up from the coffee table and holding it between the hockey game and Ratso's face.

'Oh, I forgot to tell you, I guess. That's a guy I hired to look into this a while back. Robert McLane. I'm sorry. He's off the case now. I should've told you, Kinkstah.'

'You're goddamn right you should've told me.'

'Anyway, he didn't find anything and I guess I never paid him.'

'There's a shocker.'

'You want to call the guy, go ahead. Use the phone in the bedroom. Compare notes or whatever. Tell him the check's in the mail.'

I took the PI's bill and headed for the bedroom, just a little surprised at Ratso. Just a little surprised. The auditory aspect of the hockey game came roaring to life just as I was closing the bedroom door. Ratso had been a rather repellent friend of mine for over twenty years. It stood to reason he was going to make a rather repellent client.

Ten minutes later I came out of the bedroom and I suppose my face and demeanor told the story, because it's a rare occasion when Ratso kills the sound on a hockey game twice in one afternoon.

'What'd you find out?' Ratso said.

I took a patient puff on the cigar and exhaled a thick plume of smoke in the general direction of the polar bear's head.

'Did you compare notes with the guy?' Ratso wanted to know.

'No, I did not compare notes with the guy,' I said, 'and there's a very good reason for it.'

'What's the reason?' said Ratso.

I put the invoice back on the coffee table and walked over to the window beside the Virgin Mary. The cigar smoke appeared to be making a nice little blue-gray halo around her head, but I didn't pay her too much attention.

'Because he's dead,' I said.

NINE

*

Three days later I stood at my kitchen window, looking over a cloud-shrouded Vandam Street and feeling a great spiritual kinship with Robert Louis Stevenson, who spent the last years of his life cut off from the rest of the world in voluntary exile on Samoa. I felt a certain sartorial kinship with Stevenson as well, since I was wearing a sarong and my faithful purple bathrobe and Stevenson perpetually wore a long dark blue velvet housecoat over his pajamas even when greeting formally dressed visitors who'd come to meet the great man.

'He had a pet mouse, you know,' I said to the cat. 'He lived in Hawaii for a while on Waikiki Beach before any hotels were there and before ninety-seven Japanese tourists were waiting to make a land assault upon every elevator. Before Stevenson went to sleep each night he'd take out his flute and play a little Scottish tune, and this little mouse would come out from wherever he was hiding and dance around the room. By all records, Stevenson was one of the world's worst flute players but it didn't seem to bother him or the mouse.'

The story didn't seem to bother the cat much either. She sat stoically on the windowsill and let it roll by with the clouds.

'Stevenson loved the Samoan people and they loved him, calling him Tusitala, which means teller of tales. Though he died almost exactly a hundred years ago, there is a Samoan song that is still sung to the captains of arriving ships. The song at one point inquires if Mr Robert Louis Stevenson is aboard the ship.'

The cat, at last, seemed to be paying attention to my narrative. Her eyes appeared to have changed slightly, I noticed, from their normal green perpetual pinwheels of malice to placid green pools of reflection in which I could see the sadness in my own face. It was not just a sadness for Stevenson; it was a wistful state of melancholia that I felt for my old friend Ratso and for myself.

For the past three days I'd tried in vain to learn more about McLane, the PI Ratso had hired who'd so recently gone to Jesus. The phone number I'd called from Ratso's apartment had now been disconnected. The small agency he'd run had also seemed suddenly to blip off the screen. The lawyer, Moie Hamburger, according to his secretary, was out of the country on an extended vacation. Perhaps Ratso had not been totally open with me about the situation, but clearly something was going on that neither of us understood. Some little prickling inner sense told me that he was in danger. I had a sick, persistent feeling that far from his finding his mother, something horrible might find him first. And there was nothing I could do but smoke a cigar and talk to a cat.

'Rambam's grudging help,' I continued, 'will also not be forthcoming in the foreseeable future. He left a message on the machine this morning from the airport that he's on his way to Hong Kong to investigate a slip-and-fall accident aboard a junk for a lawyer in Seattle. After that, he says, he's apparently jumping through his asshole with the paratroopers from the Burmese Airborne Battalion. There's a nice bunch of fellows to be jumping with.'

The cat jumped off the windowsill and landed on the kitchen table without a parachute. She did not care a fig about politics or governments and she liked Rambam only slightly better than she liked Ratso, which is to say not a hell of a lot.

'Anyway, we've reached an apparent dead end in the case here in New York. There's no one to investigate and no one to advise me what to do. The only other private investigator I could go to for advice is now living in California. Name's Kent Perkins. He's a big ol' good-natured Texas boy. I think you'd like him. He used to refer to his penis as "the Spoiler".'

The cat gave a little mew of distaste.

'Anyway, I left him a message but I haven't heard back from him.'

I walked over to the espresso machine, which was now giving forth a fairly decent racket and drew myself a hot, steaming cup that tasted almost as bitter as my current attitude toward this case. I paced back and forth in the drafty old loft, puffing the cigar and sipping the espresso and carrying on a one-sided conversation with myself or the cat or some silent witness. Ratso's mother, for all I knew. It wasn't very healthy really and it made me feel kind of paranoid.

'There's nothing wrong with a man talking at great length to a cat,' I said to the cat, who was now chasing a cockroach around the far corner of the kitchen counter. 'Besides, I talked to Bellevue Hospital yesterday and the bad news is that their records don't go back that far. The good news is that they didn't ask me to come in for observation.'

I glanced quickly at the cat, who was now sitting on the counter staring at me. I thought I detected something akin to a form of feline empathy in her eyes. It was also possible that the cockroach had now crawled up on the wall behind me.

'So Robert Louis Stevenson,' I said, 'had been a great friend of a Samoan chieftain named Mataafa, and once he personally arranged to release many of Mataafa's followers from a wrongful imprisonment. The Samoans, quite reasonably, hated manual labor. But once the prisoners were released, they set about building a road from the town of Apia to Stevenson's house. The road, which still stands today in Samoa, was called "The Road of the Loving Hearts".'

A short while later, the cat was asleep, the street was noticeably darker, and I was still standing at the window, staring into the gloom. Ratso was one of my oldest and best friends, I thought. What the hell. If Robert Louis Stevenson, with his frail and sickly constitution, could travel from Scotland to the South Sea Islands, I figured I could certainly make a trip to Florida.

It could've been my natural curiosity that helped me make the decision. Or it could've been my own selfish pride that wouldn't allow me to admit failure once I'd taken on a job. Or possibly, the fact that I was now determined to go to Florida had nothing to do with me at all. Maybe it was much simpler than that.

'The Road of the Loving Hearts', it would seem, sometimes extends itself beyond Samoa.

TEN

*

Two days later, having ascertained from Ratso how to contact his adoptive mother once I got to Florida, I embarked upon the brief little mission that I hoped would finally shed some light on the identity of his biological mother. I'd pretty well come to the conclusion that the safe deposit box his father had mentioned to his mother was the only lead I had left. If the cupboard turned up bare in Florida, I figured, Ratso was going to have to hire Nero Wolfe.

'And that,' I said to the cat as I packed my suitcase, 'is going to cost money.'

The cat, understandably nervous about the presence of the suitcase, didn't care a flea about anyone else's problems. If the truth be known, she would probably feel just as well had Ratso never been born. Of course, that would've made it even more difficult for me to find his mother.

Sadly, the more hopeless the case appeared to me and the more depressed I privately became about my involvement, the more upbeat and positive was Ratso's attitude.

'I know you'll find her, Kinkstah,' he'd said. 'I can tell when you're onto something.'

'Don't get your hopes up just because I'm going to Florida,' I'd said. 'We could be off on the wrong trail altogether.'

'I'd hate to think,' Ratso had said, 'that my mother was a red herring.'

When I'd packed the suitcase, I patted the cat reassuringly, fished around inside the porcelain head of Sherlock Holmes for the extra key to the loft, and headed up the stairs to Stephanie DuPont's apartment. Stephanie was a drop-dead-gorgeous five-eleven blonde I'd been establishing a rapport with over the past year to at least the point where she'd grudgingly assented to feed the cat for two days while I was away in Florida. In the past I'd left the cat with Winnie Katz, but our relationship had deteriorated dating almost exactly from the day when Stephanie and her two little dogs, Pyramus and Thisbe, walked into our lives. The sordid truth of the matter was that Winnie and I now considered ourselves rival suitors for Stephanie's affection. Whenever the lesbian dance class over my head became silent these days, I worried.

'God, nerd,' said Stephanie when she opened her door, 'what is that ridiculous hairball growing beneath your lower lip?'

I'd been experimenting lately with a slightly new formation of facial hair. Figured it'd at least go over well with the Cubans.

'I'm workin' on my white-man hater,' I said. 'What do you think?'

'Too bad,' she said. 'I was hoping it was lip cancer.'

Stephanie had a rather caustic wit about her, to put it mildly. If she hadn't been the most beautiful, smartest, sexiest, funniest, and tallest woman in the world, I doubt if anybody'd ever talk to her. But she was and they did. If they could.

'Now all you have to do,' I said, as I got out the key, 'is to feed the cat maybe once or twice a day – '

'Once.'

'Cat's not going to like that.'

'Neither am I.'

Stephanie, no doubt, still remembered the time the cat fairly shredded her beloved Maltese, Thisbe. It had been an unfortunate incident that had occurred some time ago during my rather checkered campaign to locate Uptown Judy and it hadn't exactly been brick and mortar to my relationship with Stephanie.

'It'd be nice also,' I continued, 'if you'd keep up a little presence around the loft in my absence. One idea might be to put on my cowboy hat and sit at my desk smoking a cigar late at night – '

'Stop,' she said.

37

Then she smiled incredulously. This was followed by a noise like a bubbling brook that seemed to emanate from somewhere in her throat.

'Was that a laugh?'

'I'm trying not to vomit.'

'That *was* a laugh. You know what I always say: "If you can make a woman laugh, you can take her to bed with you." '

'You know what my mother always told me?'

' "Don't go out with Jews"?'

'No,' said Stephanie DuPont, with the sultry little smile still ticcing lightly on her lips. 'She said: "Never, never, never go to bed with a man who wears a white-man hater." '

Then she kissed me lightly on the lips, just above the white-man hater, took the key from my hand, and closed the door.

'Not bad,' I said to the cat, as I walked back into the loft. 'First a Rockefeller, now a Dupont.'

ELEVEN

*

A short time later, with suitcase and cigar in hand, I was walking out the door of the loft when the phones rang. I walked back to the desk, set down my suitcase, and picked up the blower on the left.

'Start talkin',' I said.

'This is the voice of your conscience,' said the blower.

'Impossible,' I said. 'He's right here and I'm lookin' at him.' I gave a perfunctory little Nero Wolfe-like nod to Sherlock Holmes's head. His face remained impassive.

'Maybe your conscience just likes to visit Southern Califor-

nia,' drawled the friendly voice, placing a suggestive, somewhat primitive inflection on the word 'visit'.

'No self-respecting conscience would ever visit Southern
California.'

'That's why I still keep my Texas driver's license,' said Kent
Perkins.

I had a plane to catch and this little banter was getting me
nowhere, but there was something about Kent that made you
want to trust him. Maybe that's why he'd been so successful in
the PI business. Also, it was hard to dislike a guy who'd already
told you that in his will he'd left you a 1964 Lincoln Continental
with suicide doors that opened from the middle of the car
outward. It was the same model car that Kennedy had been
shot in in Dallas, but I wasn't going to let one unfortunate
incident total my karma.

Anyway, with Rambam out of the picture, Perkins was the
only experienced consultant I had to work with. The fact that
an adult referred to his penis as 'the Spoiler' was no reason to
believe that the person didn't have the knowledge and
maturity to help me with the problem at hand, so to speak. Still,
it gave one pause.

Nonetheless, I sat down at the desk, laid my cigar down
in the large, Texas-shaped ashtray, and proceeded to fill Kent
Perkins in on the details of the investigation as I knew them. I
had to admit it felt mildly reassuring to be sharing the information with someone other than my hopelessly ambivalent,
subjective, sometimes tedious, often rather repellent client.

'So what happened to the other PI?' Perkins wanted to know.
'The one Ratso hired to find his mother in the first place?'

'He went to Jesus.'

'We have a lot of that out here. People dropping whatever
else they're doing and joining up with Christian fundamentalist cults.'

I didn't say anything. Just puffed patiently on the cigar.

'That is what you mean, isn't it?' said Perkins.

'I'm afraid not,' I said.

By the time I'd cradled the blower, I was ready to change my plane reservation to Fat Chance, Arkansas. Kent Perkins had, indeed, offered his personal help. Then he had given me about seven hundred good reasons why a private investigator, especially one who's a friend of his client, should never take a case of this nature. The odds of a successful conclusion after all this time were about as good as winning the lottery, he'd said, and the work would be a lot harder. Probably, Perkins had asserted, Ratso and I would no longer be friends by the conclusion of the case. There was also the off chance I might find Ratso's mother. Then dark forces often might come into play from siblings and other relatives who felt threatened by the new relationship coming to light. Finally, Perkins had set forth from personal experience the cruelest blow of all: that Ratso, after waiting a lifetime to find his real mother, might be rejected again by her as he had most likely been in the first place.

'Well, there's nothing like a healthy negative attitude,' I said to the cat, as I picked up the suitcase. 'I envy you. Stephanie will be looking after you. I'll be back soon. Until then, you're in charge.'

Then I set out in the cold, brisk, hungover New York half-light to hail a hack for La Guardia and points south. I didn't stop feeling a certain soul chill until I was aboard the aircraft with New York City in the rearview mirror. Then I took off my overcoat for the first time.

I hadn't thought much about it but the shirt I was wearing for Florida was the one I'd bought in Hawaii several years ago. According to the guy who'd sold it to me it was an exact replica of the shirt Montgomery Clift had died in in *From Here to Eternity.* As things turned out, it was a damned near perfect sartorial choice.

TWELVE

*

I arrived in Florida in only slightly better condition than Dustin Hoffman in *Midnight Cowboy*. The pressures of living in New York, which can reduce the human spirit to rancid sandwich meat over a long weekend, combined with Kent Perkins's dire predictions about the case, had resulted in my hitting the tarmac in a fairly amphibious state. I was pleased to observe, at least, that many people at the Miami Airport were wearing white-man haters just like mine. Also, it was comforting to note that the vast majority of the people there were extremely o-l-d. It made me feel almost youthful. Kind of like a dead teenager. Whatever else you could say about the place, the demographics were good.

Tony Bruno, an old friend of mine from the days I was living in the tow-away zone known as Los Angeles, had once told me that there were over six hundred different kind of palm trees in the world and almost all of them had been imported and now grew in Florida. Unfortunately, most of them now seemed to be lined up in front of one kind of mall. I waved at them from my rent-a-car and they waved back along with a guy who looked like he was either the junta-appointed president of Haiti or your yard-man. I didn't have the time to find out which. When you're driving a rent-a-car in Miami, you want to be on your way.

I wasn't sure how many krauts had had their vacations rather abruptly terminated while driving rent-a-cars in Miami, but I knew it was a sizable number. The mills of the Lord grind slowly but they grind exceedingly fine. In fact, for the past few years now when, in my travels, I've come across a party of German tourists someplace I've always made it a matter of conscience to approach their table with a friendly, innocent,

41

American smile and say: 'Have you checked out Miami?' None of them have found much humor in this. But it could be because they're Dutch or Swiss. The problem, of course, is somewhat complicated by the fact that if the tourist party had indeed been of the German persuasion, humor not being their particular long suit, they wouldn't have gotten the joke anyway. They never do.

I banished all dark thoughts from my mind as I zimmed along in my rent-a-car to pick up Ratso's mother at the Golden Flamingo Retirement Center, which was pretty near the airport. That was a good thing, because I'd forgotten to wrap my lunch in a road map. I hadn't driven a rent-a-car since Christ was a cowboy, but I found it to be a very exhilarating experience. After the first few miles you cease to care about the welfare of your vehicle, yourself, or anyone else in the world.

I passed by palm trees and parking meters and colorful shirts and sunshine glinting brightly off of every fast-food franchise under heaven. A carefree, pastel, old-time color postcard rent-a-view that made you wonder whether Cerberus, that three-headed dog of crime, greed, and ecological disaster was still guarding the gate. In Miami, as in life, staring too intently at the façade may be harmful to the eyes. Staring too intently behind it, of course, is unthinkable. I found myself whistling 'England Swings' as I drove along and once again came to the conclusion that the world is divided into two groups of people: those who like Roger Miller and those who don't.

The Golden Flamingo Retirement Center looked like any other condo-apartment lobby-type setup except for the mandatory mental-hospital sign that stated: Today is THURSDAY. The next meal is LUNCH. This, of course, was necessary for many of the occupants of the center, the dates on whose cartons, unfortunately, had expired. There seemed to be an atmosphere of moderately restrained excitement around the place, and it didn't take me long to find out the reason: Perry Como was coming. There was a comforting, almost seductive, quality about the whole operation and I was kind of sorry I couldn't stick around and at least catch the show. Maybe sometime.

Lilyan Sloman was sitting out on the veranda feeding the birds and scanning a back issue of *National Lampoon*, which her son, Ratso, had once edited. I took one look at her and realized that far from being out where the buses don't run, she had her wits collected about her in a manner more meticulous than were my own, which, of course, wasn't saying all that much.

'Sit down, Kinky,' she said, as casually as an old lover. 'It's been a long time.'

'Yes, it has,' I said, pulling up a deck chair. I was racking my brains trying to remember the few times I'd met Lilyan, and the job wasn't made easier by the fact that I'd been by and large cookin' on another planet for most of the previous decade.

'How's Larry?' she said, looking at me with a mother's eyes.

'Larry's fine,' I said. 'I think he just wants to put an end to not knowing. He wants once and for all to find out the truth. The last thing he told me before I left was: "I just want to spank this monkey and put it to bed." '

Lilyan laughed. 'That sounds like him,' she said. 'But I'm just worried that he may not realize that the monkey's already been sleeping for a long, long time. By the time it finally wakes up it may have become a big, hairy ape. He might not like that.'

'Or,' I said, as I watched an old man practicing his croquet shots, 'it might turn out to be a big, hairy steak, in which case Ratso *would* like it.'

'He *is* eating?' Ratso's mother asked me earnestly. She was probably the only person in the world who knew Ratso and could ask that question without getting laughed out of town.

'Let's put it this way, Lilyan,' I said. 'My initial plan to send him to that anorexia clinic in Canada has not required implementation at this time.'

'That's good,' she said, nodding to herself, then returning an ageless smile and a little wave to the man with the croquet mallet. It was a small gesture but it had in it all the shy, unmistakably ingenuous spirit of two young people meeting at their first garden party. I'd been at the party myself once, and so had Lilyan, but she'd gone for a sixty-year ride with a boy who had a car and now she was back on her own. I'd left to get cigarettes decades ago and was still standing in the checkout line behind a large Hispanic woman. In my mind I could hear Lesley Gore singing a slight paraphrasal of her song over the in-store Muzak system: 'It's my party, I can leave if I want to.' I'd left all right, and it didn't seem like I was going to be coming back anytime soon.

I watched Lilyan Sloman feeding the birds for a while. Then I watched the old guy playing croquet on a lawn as green as a cemetery. Then Lilyan and I looked at each other.

'Well,' she said, 'let's go to the bank.'

THIRTEEN

*

A short while later, after Lilyan Sloman had excused herself to change out of her summery frock into a dark, more businesslike outfit, she returned holding a little key to the bank safe deposit box.

'I could take the key down there myself, Lilyan,' I said. 'You don't really have to go with me.'

'It'll be better if I do,' she said. 'I know bankers, and when they see a young man from out of state with that cowboy hat and cigar holding the key to a little old lady's safe deposit box, it'll take more than a phone call to straighten things out.'

'They didn't like Pretty Boy Floyd either,' I said, as I helped her into the rent-a-car.

I turned out of the drive and at the same time turned the

44

conversation from bankers to lawyers by asking Ratso's mother about Moie Hamburger's father, the man who handled the adoption proceedings so many years ago. The result was illuminating, and her composure appeared to ever so slightly unravel as she spoke.

'There was always something so strange about that whole business,' she said, letting the thought hang in the sultry air for a long while.

'The adoption?'

'The adoption, the lawyer himself, the agency that sent us the baby – '

'Ratso said he thought it was a Jewish adoption agency.'

'It *was* Jewish, but there was something about the whole affair that I always felt wasn't quite – '

'Kosher?' I offered.

'That wasn't exactly the word I was looking for,' she said.

'No,' I said. 'I guess not.'

We rode along in silence for a while. I noticed her handkerchief coming out of her purse occasionally as she blew her nose and occasionally dabbed at her eyes.

'I just want Larry to be happy,' she said.

'Then you're doing the right thing by helping us get to the bottom of this.'

'No. I just feel in my heart – I have for a long time – that there may be some awful secret lurking there in the past – '

'Don't be silly. You're Larry's mother – the only one he's ever known. He loves you. But this is just something he feels he has to know.'

'The only one who knew what is in that safe deposit box was Jack. He never told me. I never wanted to know. I still don't.'

As we pulled into the parking lot of the bank, I knew I was very close to holding in my hands a crucial piece of the puzzle, just as Lilyan Sloman was also holding my hand and very close to tears. We'd worked out a deal. She'd see that I got past the phalanx of bankers into the safe deposit vault without severe blows to anything but my ego. Then, when the vault clerk and I were safely within the holy of holies, each with our respective little keys, she would have the bank officer call a taxi and she would leave.

Like any adoptive mother who'd spent her life loving and raising a son, she probably felt she was close to losing a part of him forever to his 'real' mother. Like my own mother, who was no longer alive, she just wanted her son to be happy. Like any mother's son, I hugged Lilyan Sloman until the tears stopped flowing. Then we walked into the bank like Frank and Jesse James.

The vault teller, who held one of the two keys necessary to open any safe deposit box, was in an interesting position in life. He had the power to partially unlock your gold and silver, your most cherished possessions, the secrets of your honeymoon, and yet he could never luxuriate in that wealth, never have knowledge of those secrets. The key he held, I thought very fleetingly as he inserted it into the top of the box, might well be the key to happiness.

'Okay,' he said. 'Now you put yours in.'

'That's what she told me last night,' I said.

He made a forced, rather unpleasant twitch with his lips that looked like he might be experiencing gas. Then, with his key in the box and his power diminished, the energy seemed to flow out of his body and he quietly scuttled from the room. I was all alone with Ratso's past and quite possibly Ratso's future, and it seemed very damned eerie. The key in my hand felt like Benjamin Franklin had just tied it to the end of his kite. What the hell, I thought. I didn't come down here to shake hands with Donald Duck.

I opened the box.

FOURTEEN

*

As a friend of mine in Australia once put it: 'I was drier than a nun's nasty.' I was sitting at the counter of a little Cuban bar and restaurant somewhere along the way to the airport. In my coat pocket, next to what I sometimes liked to refer to as my heart, was a yellowed, rather innocuous-looking, sealed envelope that, if I didn't miss my bet, hadn't been opened in over forty-seven years. Anything that had waited that long could wait for me to have a drink.

The bar was kind of seedy and kind of empty but it looked like I felt. The music sounded like the kind Hank Williams might've played when he was hanging out with Jack Ruby in Havana in the days before he went to Jesus, and I do not mean that he joined a Christian fundamentalist cult. Aside from wearing white-man haters to a degree that would've made Frank Zappa proud, the Cubans have many other good qualities: they're passionate and fiery-tempered, they appreciate good cigars, and they always stock their bars with about ninety-seven different kinds of rum. I ordered a large neat glass of Mount Gay Rum and a Coca-Cola on the side in honor of Timothy B. Mayer, who first recognized the power and import-ance of separating the rum from the Coke. The drink was known as the Timster and the Timster himself drank a hell of a lot of Timsters with me before he, too, went to Jesus and I went back to Texas, which many New Yorkers consider to be almost as bad.

When the two glasses arrived I drank a little rum, a little Coke, a little rum, a little Coke, a little rum, a little Coke, until there was no rum left but still a lot of Coca-Cola. There will always be a lot of Coca-Cola in the world.

I told the bartender my glass was crying and he poured out

another shot of Mount Gay. By this time I was feeling much better and had just about decided to slit open the envelope and then slit open Ratso's throat if it contained Jack Sloman's old collection of baseball cards.

I got out the envelope and set it down on the bar next to the glass of Mount Gay. It was a moment fraught with destiny, and I was the only one in the place who realized it. In fact, I was very damn near the only one in the place. The jukebox had suddenly gone autistic on me and the bartender had taken to swatting the occasional fly like the guy in *Casablanca* with the funny hat. Maybe it was the calm before the storm.

I picked up the envelope off the bar and my friend's fate was literally in my hands. A little rum, a little Coke, a little rum, a little Coke and I heard a voice sneaking up on me like a Miskito Indian and whispering in my ear. It sounded a lot like Lilyan Sloman. It said: 'I never wanted to know. I still don't.'

'You're right,' I said, as the bartender swatted a fly.

Then I heard another voice. It was kind of staticy and distant but not without certain natural elements of the ring of truth. An overseas call in a dream. It was the Timster's voice. It said: 'The envelope, please.'

'You're right, too,' I said, and I opened the envelope.

FIFTEEN

*

I was envisioning Stephanie DuPont bending over to feed the cat, the envelope was safely ensconced in my breast pocket, and I was dutifully watching for occasional weirdly placed signs depicting an aircraft taking off, when I picked up a Miskito Indian sneaking up in the rearview mirror of the rent-a-car.

Upon closer inspection it looked like a krautmobile of some type but with all the four-wheeled penises out there today, it's hard to tell. As is often the case, it got bigger.

It stayed right behind me for three more pictures of airplanes taking off and I was starting to become mildly agitato. Two more pictures of airplanes and I was definitely not singing 'England Swings'. Driving a rent-a-car through a strange town and being closely tailed by a dangerous-looking, large, modern krautmobile with two sinister specimens lurking behind the windscreen was like a long-buried dream fragment from a troubled adolescence suddenly exploding and lodging itself in your skull-house. The krautmobile moved menacingly closer. I just caught a glimpse of the guy in the passenger seat playing with something in his lap. I doubted seriously if it was himself.

What would James Dean have done in a situation like this, I wondered? What would Jim Rockford do? What the hell was happening to me down here in the Land of My People? I instinctively patted the breast pocket of my coat. The envelope was still there. I shot another glance at the rearview. The kraut-mobile was still there, too. It had to be the envelope. They wanted the envelope. Or else, and far worse, they wanted no one to know the information which it contained.

I cursed myself for letting the bright, mindless Florida sunshine lull me into being careless. The red flags had all been there and I must've thought it was a going-out-of-business sale. In a rather macabre fashion, maybe it was. I hadn't listened between the lines, apparently, to what both Rambam and Perkins had tried to tell me about this kind of investigation into the primeval. I'd forgotten about the guy in the black overcoat who'd tailed me in Brooklyn after I'd gotten the adoption papers from the warehouse. And what about Moie Hamburger, the son of the lawyer who'd arranged the deal, suddenly blipping off the screen? Maybe he was at the bottom of the East River right now with little gefilte fishes chasing one another through his eye sockets.

That's the way it happens, I thought, as I stared into the gaping mouth of an assault rifle that looked like it was ready to say *Ahhh*. You go on a short trip to help a friend and you leave your protective coat of good ol' New York paranoia behind. You look for answers and, incredibly enough, you even find them. Then the kraut car closes, then it pulls next to you, then the weapon rises into view like a daydream gone bad, and somewhere between the fun and the sun and the rum and the gun you follow that last airplane picture right up into the sky. A window seat to limbo if the Catholic Church is correct, where you fly a tight, tedious holding pattern through night and fog for at least a thousand years with a small Aryan child kicking the seat behind you, while next to you a fat man from Des Moines is locked in a hideous rictus of eternal vomiting upon the half-completed crossword puzzle that is all of our lives.

The other passengers to limbo, if the Catholic Church is correct, are non-baptized babies, all of whom cry incessantly for their mothers throughout the thousand-year vector. Whether said mothers are biological or adoptive raises an interesting legal point, for by the time the plane lands every family tree on earth has been totally defoliated and no one cares a thousand-year-old Chinese egg whether the sign on the terminal reads HEAVEN: NO SMOKING OR HELL: NOTHING TO DECLARE.

And then, lo and behold, a miracle had occurred. Traffic was suddenly slowing to a crawl and a Florida highway patrolman was stopping all cars beside a large sign that read: DRUG INTERDICTION CHECKPOINT AHEAD. I was so happy to have Big Brother watching over me I was about ready to hum a few bars of 'The Love Song of J. Edgar Hoover'. I stopped the rent-a-car and cautiously glanced over my shoulder.

There was a scurry of frenzied activity in the krautmobile now as it suddenly roared across the grass divider, performed a mud-slinging, gravel-gouging L.A. turn-around, and shot off in the opposite direction with several black-and-whites on its tail. The cavalry had arrived.

As for me, I exhibited the even-minded patience of the great Mahatma while the highway patrolman checked my driver's license and asked routine questions and a large German shepherd sniffed around the floorboards and the backseat area. I didn't mind. I had lots of time now. I also had the license plate number of the krautmobile just in case good German engineering carried the day.

While the highway patrol continued with their investigation, I realized with some little satisfaction that mine was in large part over. With the information I now had, the wrapping-it-up aspect should be child's play. Today would be an important day in the history of Larry 'Ratso' Sloman. The search for his mother, I felt, was all but over, along with the uncertainty, the insecurity, and the nagging doubt he'd carried with him most of his adult life. Quite literally, he was now a different man. And he didn't even know it yet.

I sat back in the driver's seat, lit up a cigar, and smiled through the open window at the nearby grove of citrus trees, the sun-dappled skyline, and the white gulls wheeling to and fro across the brush-stroke horizon of the kind of blue that seems to change ever so slightly in your imagination like half-remembered, half-closed eyes.

'You want to pop your trunk for us, sir?' the patrolman was saying.

'Well,' I said, 'there goes a hundred kilos of Peruvian marching powder.'

'We don't appreciate jokes about drugs, sir.'

'There's no drugs in the trunk,' I said, pushing the button that opened it. 'There's just my wife.'

'We don't appreciate jokes about that either,' he said, letting the 'sir' slide, and walking around to the back of the car.

A moment later he returned and waved me on my way, his face young, impassive, unsmiling, like a slightly bored eagle scout.

'Let me ask you one question, Officer,' I said. 'What kind of jokes do you guys appreciate?'

'Well,' he said, 'you're from New York. You wouldn't want to know about it.'

'I just live in New York. I'm actually from Texas.'

'Then you really wouldn't want to know about it,' he said.

SIXTEEN

*

An hour and a half later, from a pay phone at Miami International Airport, I called a familiar number in New York. I was delighted to find my party at home and to hear his rather raucous, rodent-like voice.

'Kinkstah!' Ratso shouted ebulliently. 'What'd you find, Kinkstah?'

'Hi, David,' I said.

There was an unusual, yet, under the circumstances, quite understandable silence on the other end of the blower. Then I heard a small, birdlike voice, in tone and timbre, possibly not terribly dissimilar to that of Ratso's father in the days before he died.

'David?' it said.

'David.'

'David,' said Ratso, still not sure he liked it. 'David.'

'Beats Goliath,' I said supportively.

'That's it? David?'

'No. There's more. Your full name is David Victor Goodman.'

'Jesus Christ.'

'I asked for it but they said that handle was taken.'

'And my mother –'

'Your mother's name was Mary Goodman. I don't know if she's still alive, but if she is, you could be meeting her soon. Of course, earlier this afternoon I didn't know if I'd still be alive to make this phone call.'

'Does Lilyan know?'

'No one knows but you and me and Mary Goodman.'

'I'm going to call Lilyan. I don't think I'll tell her yet. Just see how she's doing.'

'That'd be thoughtful,' I said. 'I wish I could call my mother, too. I just don't know the area code.'

'You talk to her more than you know, Kinkstah.'

'I hope to God you're right.'

'I'm always right,' said Ratso. 'Especially to have a friend like you.'

'Don't lay it on too thick,' I said, leaning away from the phone to check the departure board. When I put the blower next to my eardrum again Ratso was in the midst of some kind of frenetic Jewish Hare Krishna chant.

'Daaavid Victah Goodman! Daa-vid Vic-tah Goodman! DavidVictahGoodman!'

The thought of Ratso dancing around his cluttered apartment shouting his new name to the stuffed polar bear's head was enough to make me smile for a moment, which is something you don't see too often at Miami International Airport. Sometimes good, solid amateur detective work can be its own reward. If Ratso's your client, of course, it's the only one you're probably ever going to get.

'Just think,' shouted Ratso. 'I might be Steve Goodman's twin brother, accidentally separated at birth!'

'Or you might be Benny Goodman's twin brother, accidentally separated at birth.'

'Or I might even be related to the Goodman of Goodman, Schwerner, and Cheney,' said Ratso.

Just in case you were jumping rope in the schoolyard at the time, or using rope for other purposes, Goodman, Schwerner, and Cheney were three young civil rights workers who were killed by the Klan in Mississippi in the early sixties. Cheney was black, but Goodman and Schwerner were two Jewish kids from Queens, where Ratso was from, who went down South in the cause of freedom and equality. Abbie Hoffman, too, was down in Mississippi at about that time, and the early civil rights movement, it should be noted, was generously infused with Jewish blood, if, indeed, there is such a thing. It should also be noted that good little white Christian church workers were few and far between at that particular place at that particular time. This is not really surprising, for the dangerous role of the troublemakers in history has often fallen to the Jewish people. Anne Frankly, it should be noted, in passing, that a great deal of good for the advancement of mankind has been accomplished between circumcision, where they cut off the tip of your dick, to crucifixion, where they throw the whole Jew away.

'It'd be an honor,' I said, 'to have been related to *that* Goodman.'

'The trouble is,' said Ratso, 'today most people probably think Goodman, Schwerner, and Cheney were a law firm.'

'Today,' I said, 'they probably would be a law firm. Besides, I'm going to miss my plane.'

'You know the Goodman I'd *really* like to be related to?' said Ratso, totally oblivious of another American attempting to board an aircraft.

'I can't imagine,' I said, as I looked around nervously for the gate.

'The Goodman I'd *really* like to be related to –'

'Goddamn it, Ratso, spit it! I'm going to miss my plane.'

Ratso paused maddeningly. When he spoke again it was in a tone of great and careless dignity.

'It's just possible,' he said, 'that I'm an heir to the Goodman Egg Noodle fortune.'

There was nothing left to say. And, quite fortunately, there was no time left to say it.

SEVENTEEN

*

I goose-stepped to the gate just in time to hop a big silver bird flying North. I took an aisle seat somewhere in its lower intestine. It was time, I figured, as I went through the wheels-up experience, to stop patting myself on the back and start looking for Mary Goodman. Unfortunately, there were about 64 million Mary Goodmans on the East Coast. By the time I'd completed the laborious process of contacting all of them, Ratso would probably be in the Shalom Retirement Village himself, refusing to wear trousers and insisting others address him as Admiral Hornblower.

If baby Ratso had come through the offices of a Jewish adoption agency, as I now believed, the old files of temples and synagogues might be good places to start. Jews usually keep pretty methodical records. The Old Testament, which is, in large part, a somewhat glorified seed catalogue of who begat whom, who cast his seed upon the ground, and who merely coveted his neighbor's ass, has been around for thousands of years.

Now that we knew the name of the subject, we might be able to turn up an old address that could possibly be very helpful in running down her current whereabouts. Unless, of course, the building had become a state prison, a McDonald's, or a parking lot, or some other aspect of man's progress had taken place.

Kent Perkins, I remembered, had suggested I check the public library for old telephone directories from the forties. If that approach didn't work, he'd offered to get involved himself and try to locate her through CD-ROM, which was something I viewed almost as suspiciously as an Australian aboriginal might regard the little device you put inside your dumper that turns the water blue.

Of course, it would all be worth it if in the end we found Ratso's mother. Especially, I thought, if she turned out to be the Goodman of the Goodman Egg Noodle fortune. At least then, when it came time to send Ratso his bill, I might not find myself hosed to the barnyard door.

I drifted off into a fitful sleep and dreamed one of those ridiculous dreams that nobody pays any attention to because it often tells us a little more than we wish to know about ourselves. In the dream I was dressed in the same blue velvet housecoat that Robert Louis Stevenson had worn through a lifetime of ill health and convalescence. I was inside a huge mansion walking across miles and miles of bathroom tiles to open the front door. Behind me, in the glittering dining room, the Goodman Egg Noodle people were having a dinner party for the Rockefellers and the DuPonts. The entree, served, of course, upon a four-poster bed of Goodman's Egg Noodles, appeared to be a goose. When the servant, who looked very much like Supreme Court Justice Clarence 'Frogman' Thomas, cut the goose with a big, gleaming knife, inside the goose was a duck and inside the duck was a chicken, and inside the chicken was a pheasant, and inside the pheasant was a squab, and inside the squab was a quail.

I never found out what was inside the quail, because the knocking on the door grew louder and I had to go open it.

Outside in the snow was a man wearing a coonskin cap with the head of the animal attached to the front, its eyes sewn shut. He wore a pimp's flashy overcoat, a shirt that looked like it had once belonged to Engelbert Humperdinck, a pair of lox-colored pants, and red shoes that I intuitively knew had once been worn by someone who was no longer with us. He also wore a big, good-natured smile. As I ushered him to the table, no one appeared to take the slightest notice of his presence.

Suddenly, Mary Goodman, who strongly resembled Nancy

Reagan auditioning for *Daughter of Dr Jekyll*, stood up and began emitting a strange Palestinian keening noise. The stranger looked at her with tragic, disbelieving eyes.

'Mom?' he said.

'We don't want him!' she screamed. 'Send him away!'

I ushered the pitiable creature back out into the snow. Before I closed the door, he turned and put his hand on my shoulder.

'Thanks a lot for helping me, pal,' he said. His eyes swirled like little sad Jacuzzis.

As he walked away I noticed that he was wearing the Robert Louis Stevenson coat and I was now attired in the formal outfit of a butler. I felt guilty, but I didn't know the nature of the crime. All I knew was I was the butler and I'd done it. I woke from the dream to find a small Aryan child kicking the back of my seat.

The rest of the flight, as they say, was uneventful. It was late by the time I got into the city, but the night was clear and a silver sliver of moon was playing hide-and-seek with me between the skyscrapers. The air felt even colder than when I'd left, but it could've been nerves. Coming back to New York is almost as hard as leaving it.

The cab spit me out at 199B Vandam Street. I paid the driver, got my suitcase out of the trunk, and let myself in through the big metal door of the old converted warehouse. I took the freight elevator up to the fourth floor and was just crossing the dusty little hallway to the door of my loft when it suddenly opened.

Stephanie DuPont stood framed in the doorway and I knew right away that something was amiss. Tall, strong, beautiful women seem to collapse into little girls faster than anyone else when something is seriously wrong. I could see it in her eyes, in her hands, and certainly in the way she threw her arms around me and practically pulled me into the room.

My first thought was that something had happened to the cat. But the cat was sleeping on my desk under her sunlamp.

'You got a call just a moment ago,' Stephanie said, in a voice I almost didn't recognize. 'I heard it on the machine. A police detective – Cooperman, I think. He said it was urgent, so I picked up the phone. He said he was at the apartment and you should get over there now – '

'Where? What apartment?'

'I don't want to be the one to tell you,' she whispered like a child. Her hand reached up to smooth her hair and her hand was shaking. I grabbed the hand and held it tight.

'What did he say?'

'It's your friend Ratso,' she said. 'He was murdered tonight.'

EIGHTEEN

*

Robert Louis Stevenson, during his extended stay in the South Seas, grew to love the Polynesian people, and came to believe they were the brightest, happiest, most beautiful race to populate the earth since the ancient Greeks. Stevenson felt that the white man had cut short their cultural progress before the Polynesians were able to come forth with their own Homer and their own Socrates. He wrote many letters to the Queen and the British High Commissioner on behalf of his friend Mataafa and his followers, never realizing that the British, the Germans, and the Americans had already divided up Samoa amongst themselves and sealed its fate forever.

Many years later, Don Ho echoed Stevenson's hopes for the people of the South Seas and described how he felt those hopes had been dashed in large part by the American missionaries. 'The missionaries told the people,' said Ho, 'to bow their heads and pray. By the time they looked up, their land was gone.'

Now, as I gazed numbly out of the window of the cab, I knew in my heart that a great many pieces of my life were gone, too. The South Seas of Robert Louis Stevenson were merely a divertive device to temporarily keep the tragic chords of truth from coming back, dull and relentless, as if I were a child all dressed up and trying to understand my first funeral.

As we turned off West Broadway onto Prince Street I saw the plain-wrapped squad cars and the meat wagon, sometimes referred to as 'Hamburger Helper', parked in front of Ratso's building. They looked like dim mechanical sharks hovering in a circle of gloom.

'If this is a movie,' I said, 'I want my money back.'

The driver gave me a shopworn smile. 'That'll be four dollars and seventy-five cents,' he said.

I paid him with my subconscious mind and got out of the hack. I stood for a moment on the curb and looked at Ratso's street in the cold and crystal-clear lamplight, and time seemed suspended, as if I were standing inside a historical tableau waiting for a man with a candle to stumble in or three wise guys or somebody who'd come to bury Caesar. Maybe that was my job, I thought.

For the next few hours I only recalled certain images, as if God had significantly reduced the wattage of my powers of observation until all of life was no more than a child's kaleidoscope on a gloomy day. If there was a God. Not only was my visual prowess somewhat impaired, but I kept hearing Robert Louis Stevenson's 'Requiem' inside my head. The poem marks Stevenson's grave on top of Mount Vaea in Samoa. How it got itself over to New York so fast and inside my head was a mystery to me. Possibly it had traveled along the Road of the Loving Hearts.

> *Under the wide and starry sky.*
> *Dig the grave and let me lie.*

He certainly wasn't writing about New York, I thought, as I

mumbled my name to a uniform at the door of the building and he nodded me in. Ratso's bum was nowhere to be seen. Handouts were going to be harder now.

> *Glad did I live and gladly die*
> *And I laid me down with a will.*

Where there's a will, there's a lawyer, I thought as I walked through the hallway and waited for the little elevator. Only I didn't know where the hell the lawyer was. I just knew that he figured into all of this and all of this figured into all of whatever I was about to see upstairs.

The elevator came and I got aboard. It was a sad little elevator in a sad little world and it needed to go a lot higher than the sixth floor or a lot lower than the lobby, I reckoned, if it was ever going to catch up with Ratso.

The sixth floor was swarming with cops. Cops in uniform, plainclothes dicks, techs, good cops, bad cops, all with something slightly predatory or worse glinting deep behind their eyes as they moved to the ever-popular music of murder. Whether their job was wrapping up bundles of blood and gore into body bags and tossing them into meat wagons or lurking in some godforsaken hallway in the early hours of the dawn, drinking black coffee from Styrofoam cups, they liked their work. There's nothing wrong with a cop being a cop. It's just the way of their people. I took a hard right at the elevator and walked down the little hallway until I reached Ratso's door. It was open. No reason for him to ever triple-lock it again.

> *This be the verse you grave for me:*
> *Here he lies where he longed to be;*

Ratso was lying face down on the floor. A small wading pool of semi-coagulated blood was all around the upper half of his body. It was the color of pink horseradish.

A photographer and some other kind of technician were still futzing around with his body. Taking pictures of his garish outfit. A nice close-up of the red antique shoes he was wearing that had once belonged to a dead man. Now they had walked full circle.

> Home is the sailor, home from the sea,
> And the hunter home from the hill.

Detective Sergeant Fox and a cop I didn't know were at Ratso's little desk riffling through his phone book and bank statements and listening to his answering machine. 'Where are you?' a rather seductive female voice was asking. 'I've been waiting here at the Pink Pussycat for over two hours.' Fox chuckled to himself.

I looked up and saw Sergeant Mort Cooperman standing by the windows beside the statue of the Virgin Mary. They both looked grim. Cooperman shook his head at me sadly and shrugged a cop shrug. The Virgin Mary looked right at me and didn't say a thing. She'd seen it all before.

'Don't look at his face, Tex,' said Cooperman. 'He's not ready for his close-up yet.'

There was an uncomfortable silence. I continued staring at the Virgin Mary. One of us was bound to blink soon.

'If it's any consolation,' Cooperman said, 'he was dead before he hit the floor.'

'Some guys have all the luck,' I said.

NINETEEN
*

It is a rather ironic fact, but those familiar with the world of crime will swear that it's true. When no killer and no weapon are found at the scene, the murderer most often turns out to be the person closest to the victim in life – the spouse, the best friend, the family member, the person who called the police in the first place or possibly helped in some way with the investigation. While every cop knows this and it may make a good rule of thumb in crime solving, it does represent somewhat of a spiritual indictment of the human race. In other words, to know us is to love us. Maybe it is that we've just never been very good at one-on-one.

It was not surprising, therefore, that despite Cooperman's ostensibly sympathetic approach to the questioning, he nonetheless regarded me as a primary suspect. I was in a state of cultural mayonnaise at the time, and this was not improved by my witnessing Ratso being taken away in a body bag. One of the best friends I'd ever had was suddenly, surreally, worm bait, and now Cooperman and I were sitting on this rather sordid sofa conversing like two Chinese towkays haggling over the price of fish maws.

Strangely enough, I remember our conversation quite clearly, almost like clinical recall. Cooperman was smoking a Gauloise and lighting it with a Zippo and a vulture-like twist of his thick neck. I was smoking a cigar and lighting it with a kitchen match and a prayer. The smoke along with the Virgin Mary being there reminded me somehow of incense. If incense was supposed to spiritually cleanse a place, I remember thinking it had better get on the stick.

The dull grief that was beginning to manifest itself in my heart soon drove the Requiem for Ratso verses out of my head. And in some dark train yard of my brain, I suppose a coupling was already taking place between Ratso's murder and the now seemingly rather pointless search for his mother. Whether the two were connected I couldn't say for sure, but Cooperman was having none of it. He started the grilling off in his own inimitable, blunt, straight-ahead style. For matters of brevity, I've recorded only a small portion of our conversation here.

'Did Ratso own a sawed-off?'

'A sawed-off what?'

'Shotgun.'

'Not to my knowledge.'

'Do you own a sawed-off shotgun, Tex?'

'Not to my knowledge.'

'I thought all you cowboys rode horses and carried guns.'

'I don't have a gun and I only ride two-legged animals.'

'When was the last time you talked to your buddy?'

'Earlier this evening. I called him around seven from the Miami airport.'

'And you were down there looking for – '

'Ratso's birth mother. His adoptive father had died recently – '

'Did you find his mother?'

'No. But I learned her name. Mary Goodman.' Here Cooperman jotted down a little note on his pad.

'How did Ratso sound when you talked to him?'

'Excited. He thought he'd soon be meeting his real mother.'

'Maybe he already has.'

'Maybe.'

Cooperman killed his cigarette and promptly lit another one. I dropped a Clarence Darrow-sized ash in the little ashtray. I looked up at the photo of Ratso meeting Nixon. Ratso with Bob Dylan. Who was going to finish the Abbie Hoffman book now? I wondered. Ratso'd only been working on it for five years. Of course, he could interview Abbie himself now. That would be a scoop.

'Did he ever get into arguments, say, over matters of money or women?'

'Yes and yes.'

'Start with money. When'd he have an argument about money?'

'Every time he ever got out of a cab.'

'I see.'

'No you don't. The guy had fishhooks in his pockets. The

63

whole time I've known him I don't think he's ever picked up the check. But this is not the kind of behavior that causes your piece to be taken off the board. Maybe it was just a basic form of neurotic Judaism in action. At heart, and in life, however, Ratso was always a man of very generous spirit. One of the kindest, most gentlehearted people I've ever known.'

'Then why does somebody ice him?' Cooperman glared at me. I looked around the room for help.

'I don't know. Ask Nixon why he went along with Watergate. Ask Bob Dylan why he wrote "Mr Tambourine Man". Ask Abbie Hoffman why he videotaped his vasectomy.'

'I'm asking you.'

'And I'm telling you the only thing I can think of that makes any sense. Somebody killed him because he and I were getting close to finding his real mother.'

Cooperman gave me a tired smile. I gave him a tired smile. I was so emotionally spindled and mutilated that I was ready to accept any social intercourse I could get.

'Let me give you some advice,' said Cooperman. 'Leave the involved plots and the conspiracy theories to the Hollywood screenwriters. When this murder is solved – and it will be – it'll be a lot simpler than that and a lot closer to home. Now what about broads? He did have broads in his life, didn't he?'

'How'd you think this couch got skid-marks on it?'

'I'm gonna want the names of all his women for the past five years.'

'That's easy. Go down to the Monkey's Paw and look on the wall of the men's dumper. Anyway, you're not suggesting a woman came in here and Sam Cooked him with a sawed-off shotgun?'

'No. A man did that. The door was forced, by the way. But that don't mean some skirt didn't have it in for Ratso. Could've hired somebody to come in here and terminate him.'

I was starting to feel a physical pain in my head and my gut as the time ticked ruthlessly by and Ratso didn't walk back in and turn on a hockey game.

'I'd like to hire somebody,' I said, 'to come in here and terminate this conversation.'

'You just did,' said Cooperman, standing up and stretching his back. 'That's the crummiest sofa I've ever sat on in my life.'

'Try sleeping on it.'

'Try not leaving town,' he said, and he walked over to confer with Fox.

TWENTY
*

The death of someone close to you is never as much fun as it's cracked up to be. I should know. I've been to that rodeo on a handful of occasions and every time you get thrown it gets a little bit harder for you to pick up your hat and dust it off. In fact, four cigars and half a bottle of Jameson later, at three-thirty in the morning, as I sat at my desk in the loft playing solitaire with Ratso's adoption papers, I still was having a hell of a time believing what I'd seen with my own eyes.

I poured another shot of Jameson into the old bullhorn and watched my watch wind its world-weary way to a quarter to four. It was a death watch and it didn't really give a damn about anything but methodically monitoring the seconds, minutes, and hours of all our lives. Of moments, it knew nothing. Wristwatches were always like that, I thought. Emotionless, expressionless little faces forever keeping themselves an arm's length away from your heart.

'Next time I'll get a sundial,' I said to the cat.

The cat said nothing but sat on the desk rather protectively close to me. Through some ancient feline sonar she had perhaps sensed another sea change in my heart. She'd weathered this sort of situation before and appeared to be battening down the hatches for whatever came next. If the cat had known that it was Ratso who'd gone to Jesus, I wouldn't like to predict what she might've done. Probably she'd have donned a long, green leprechaun's cap, picked up a fiddle, and danced a jig from one red telephone to the other until the cows came home, which, in New York City, could take a while. Cats, however, like humans, can never be sure for whom the bell tolls. Unlike humans, they are usually too polite to ask.

I lifted the old bullhorn toward the living room and the old couch where Ratso had stayed when he'd been a housepest at the loft. I recited the last verse from the poem Breaker Morant had written in his cell on April 19, 1902, the night before his execution.

> Let's toss a bumper down our throat,
> Before we pass to Heaven,
> And toast: 'The trim-set petticoat
> We leave behind in Devon.'

I included Breaker's last words that he shouted at the British firing squad: 'Shoot straight, you bastards!'

I killed the shot, listened hopefully for the lesbian dance class, which wasn't there, puffed on the cigar for a while, and killed that, too. Then I killed the light and went to bed. It was enough killing for one day.

The sandman, it seemed, was on sabbatical and that gave me no choice but to painfully toss and turn the sad situation over in my aching mind. I did not agree with Cooperman that a 'trim-set petticoat' was responsible for Ratso's death. Nor did I believe he'd been whacked in a feud or argument over money, though I'd felt like killing him myself on several occasions for just that same reason. It was possible that money or a woman figured into it, I thought, but not as simply or as neatly as

Cooperman seemed to suspect. Whoever the agent of Ratso's death was, I strongly believed he'd been set in motion forty-seven years ago, and there were only two people I could possibly think of who might be able to tell me why. Moie Hamburger and Mary Goodman. Both, unfortunately, did not appear to be eager to answer my knock on their doors of perception.

I would find Mary Goodman, I thought, if for no other reason than to tell her that her son had been looking for her. It was the least I could do for Ratso. It was the least I could do for myself. I fell asleep to the stained-glass glare of a streetlight inexorably turning red, green, yellow, and red again, like so many Popsicle saints and jukebox witches burning in the Dark Ages of the heart.

Just before dawn I began to hear a noise like a giant locust inside my pillow. In a moderately brain-dead state I collared the bedside blower and yanked it over to what I believed was my head.

'This is the AT&T operator,' said a female voice. 'You have a collect call.'

'Who's calling, operator?'

'David Victor Goodman,' she said.

TWENTY-ONE

*

When I heard the rather distinctive voice of the caller powering over the blower, I knew I'd either gone to Jesus myself or Ratso was still malingering somewhere along this mortal coil. As it became increasingly apparent that Ratso was yet among us I found myself torn simultaneously between the equally compelling twin desires of jumping for joy and killing his ass again.

'Kinkstah!' he shouted. 'Kinkstah!'

'This better be good,' I said grimly, though I must confess a virtual tidal bore of relief was washing over me. In spite of the fact that it was 5:30 A.M. and I was attempting rather unsuccessfully to disentangle my Borneo sarong from a monstro morning erection, I let out with a well-modulated Texas whoop and attempted to scoop up the cat, which irritated her no end; she stalked out of the bedroom like a disdainful lover. Of course the cat wasn't my lover. Things weren't that bad. Yet.

'I've got a problem, Kinkstah,' Ratso was saying.

'I've got one, too,' I said.

'I'm up here in Woodstock and my old friend Jack Bramson is staying at my apartment. You've met Jack, haven't you?'

'Not formally.'

'Well, he's a good guy but he's not all that reliable, if you know what I mean. Now he's not picking up the phone and my answering machine's fucked-up. I ask him to look after the place for a few days and he can't even do that.'

'Maybe you're being too hard on him.'

'Well, somebody's been fucking with my answering machine – '

'At least it's safe sex – '

'I call my number, nobody answers, and my message isn't on the machine.'

'Why does everything have to have a message these days?'

'Anyway, if you don't mind, Kinkstah, I'd like you to go over today and check the machine.'

'No can do, Rat.'

'What do you mean? After all I've done for you? I helped you find your fucking girlfriend. I helped you find that fucking cat. I helped you find the fucking Nazi – '

'What more could a fellow ask?'

'I'm serious, Kinkstah. C'mon. I'm expecting some important

calls. If Jack's there, tell him you talked to me and he'll let you in. If Jack's out, buzz the super's office and he'll give you a key.'

'Jack's out,' I said.

Once I'd laid it out for him, so to speak, it hadn't taken Ratso long to grasp the significance of the events of the previous night. His friend Jack Bramson, who resembled Ratso fairly closely in body type (what McGovern occasionally referred to as 'middle-aged Jewish meatball'), had been traveling rather light and had borrowed some of Ratso's wardrobe, which further increased the similarity. Bramson had been in the wrong place at the wrong time or, from Ratso's viewpoint, no doubt, in the right place at the right time, because if he hadn't been there Ratso at this writing would surely be shaking hands with the devil, and I do not mean urinating.

The fact that the killer had broken into the place with the express purpose of icing Ratso had not been lost upon him. He also appeared to be taking in my solemn imprecations that his life would be in grave danger once the mistake was discovered and that some careful plotting on both of our parts would be required to prevent the abrupt shortening of his life span. He still felt, however, that it was just as possible that someone wanted to unplug Jack Bramson as himself. Bramson, according to Ratso, had managed to irritate a goodly number of people in the short expanse of his star-crossed life. I didn't mention it, but Ratso, from time to time, had been rather facile at getting up a lot of people's sleeves, as well. One of those sleeves was mine.

Before I cradled the blower, I'd been able to extract a promise from Ratso that he'd stay in Woodstock until I could convince Cooperman that rumors of his death were greatly exaggerated. It worried me a bit that both Cooperman and Ratso did not share my belief that the investigation into Ratso's adoption had triggered the murder. Maybe I'd overidentified with my field of study a bit and Bramson's death was a separate matter. I certainly hoped so. Otherwise, finding Mary Goodman could become quite unpleasant.

At least Ratso was alive, I thought. Now if I could keep him that way long enough to locate his mother, I damned sure planned to turn the job over to her. For despite his outward show of bravado, I could hear in the timbre of his voice that grief and fear were lurking in the wings, and in the troubled days ahead I wasn't going to have a hell of a lot of time to hold his hand.

'You might call Lilyan in Florida,' I said. 'Before Cooperman calls her.'

'Why would he do that?'

'Because he thinks you're dead.'

'For a dead man, I took a pretty healthy dump this morning.'

'You might just keep that one to yourself,' I said.

'I have *kept* it to myself, Kinkstah,' said Ratso, with no small pride of accomplishment. 'For *four* whole days!'

TWENTY-TWO

*

The next thing on my agenda that morning, after feeding the cat and performing various personal ablutions, was the rather tricky task of calling Cooperman. Cops were funny creatures. Once they'd discovered the victim and set out on the trail of the perpetrator, they very much preferred that the victim stay dead. Cops weren't the only ones who felt this way, granting, of course, that cops felt anything. Even those of us on the peripheries of the crime-solving community shared the quite natural proclivity of desiring our worm bait to remain worm bait and not go through any complicating identity problems, sex changes, or midlife crises.

This particular problem had come very close to home with me not so long ago in a case that McGovern had aptly dubbed 'Musical Chairs'. In this decidedly convoluted adventure, the victim stubbornly refused to remain the victim, and this rather niggling recalcitrance on his part created no end of tedium for the investigator, who, unfortunately, was me. As a result, I now found myself in a position the likes of which I'd never before known in my life. I empathized with Cooperman.

I made some coffee, putting a small bit of eggshell in with the grinds as was the habit of my old pal Tom Baker. This little ritual not only enriched the flavor of the coffee but it strongly brought back an aura of the Bakerman, possibly an aura of an era. It was a strange and young and hopeful time full of rainy mornings, sunny days, and nights so grainy and raw and mystical you felt you were living inside some old French movie. Heroes, it seemed, were close enough to be your friends. Today they seem very far away. In fact, if you want to meet a real hero these days you have to find him somewhere along a dusty dream trail, evanescent as childhood, fragile as the eggshells in your coffee.

By the time I got around to calling Cooperman, the garbage trucks were grumbling, the pigeons were on the wing, the commuters had crawled through all their tunnels, and the detective sergeant himself was already out someplace in the city hot on the track of Ratso's killer. I left word with the desk sergeant for Cooperman to call me when he checked in. I had some new information on the case. That was the way I left it and it was a good thing, because when Cooperman found out I'd had a conversation with his latest murder victim the morning after the murder, he was not going to be a happy little New Yorker.

As the morning wore on, the lesbian dance class cranked up directly above my slight hangover and Stephanie DuPont

71

called at almost precisely the same time, which I took to be a good sign. She told me how sorry she was about the death of my friend and I told her that he wasn't really a friend, just a friend of a friend but the cops didn't know it yet so don't say anything to anyone, especially Pyramus and Thisbe. They'd yap it all over the neighborhood. I also told her that I couldn't say too much about the whole matter because it was getting extremely dangerous and I didn't want to drag her into it. This, of course, whetted her appetite enormously for additional information and I finally got off by promising to tell her more that evening over a couple of big, hairy steaks. Nothing like a little murder to improve your social life.

By Gary Cooper time I was beginning to experience a rather abnormal emotional state, the psychological term for which is the Swiss cheese effect. I could not remember important things like calling Sergeant Cooperman again or finding Mary Goodman before some homo erectus with a ski mask and a sawed-off shotgun found Ratso or myself. All my mind seemed to retain were trivial images floating by in a soup of the past. The cat vomiting into a carved meerschaum pipe of JFK's head, a beautiful girl in an almost empty Chinese restaurant lifting a peach-colored dress up to her waist to prove she was a true blonde (she was), Waylon Jennings pulling up in a long black limo as I was walking to the laundromat in Nashville in some other lifetime and saying: 'Get in. Walkin's bad for your image.'

Very possibly, my little trip to Florida combined with the rather hideous events of the previous night were creating a belated strain on my brain. With a conscious effort I took leave of my dawdling daydreams long enough to call Kent Perkins's answering machine in L.A. I told the machine my troubles. I related to it the latest wrinkles in the investigation. I said that I'd like for Kent to get his large, luminous buttocks out of the hot tub as soon as possible before this whole thing fell apart like a matzo ball in the rain. The machine took it all in understandingly and I felt better about myself and my life. Maybe I was just tired. I hadn't had a good night's sleep in about forty years and perhaps it was catching up with me. I crashed on the couch with the cat.

When I awoke, the sky was rather noticeably darker and the telephones were rather noticeably ringing. I navigated my way through the semi-gloom to the desk and picked up the blower on the left.

'Start talkin',' I said.

'Mit – Mit – Mit!!' said McGovern, invoking our oft-used code for the Man in Trouble hotline we'd devised when the body of a man who'd been dead for six months had been found in his Chicago apartment. Calling each other fairly regularly in this manner was merely a way to make sure that McGovern and I were both alive. So far, so good.

'Mit,' I responded rather grudgingly.

'You heard about Ratso?' he said breathlessly.

'No, but I heard that my three-year-old nephew David bit a woman on the ass in a shoe store yesterday in Silver Spring, Maryland.'

McGovern plowed doggedly on. I lit a cigar and wished I could see McGovern's face.

'Ratso's been murdered,' he said.

'Don't believe everything you read in the papers.' I laughed heartily. McGovern sounded thunderstruck.

'It's not in the papers yet. I'm just working on the story now. Wait a minute, Kinkster! What do you know that you aren't telling me?'

'I saw the body last night. Very convincing. Fooled me, in fact. But it wasn't Ratso. It was a Ratso impersonator. Friend of his who happened to be staying there for the weekend. Ratso's alive and well and just as obnoxious as ever.'

'This changes the story.'

'Yes, and if you'll help me, I might like to change it some more.'

Keeping things strictly off the record, I told McGovern about

Ratso's new identity as David Victor Goodman and about my preparing to embark upon the search for Mary Goodman. I also told him that in the very near future his help might become essential in finding Ratso's mother if other methods didn't prove successful.

'It's great to feel needed,' he said.

'Now tread carefully with this story. No mention of anything to do with the adoption investigation, and remember, the cops may still not know that the victim wasn't Ratso.'

'That's what we members of the fifth estate like to refer to as a scoop.'

'Maybe next time Cooperman will return my phone calls. I may want to assemble the Village Irregulars on this one. Of course, Downtown Judy's gone, Rambam's out of the country, and Ratso's going to have to keep a rather low profile for a while.'

'That doesn't leave much. And I wish, just between us girls, that you'd think twice about continuing to look for Ratso's mother. Obviously, the guy thought he was killing Ratso. Next time he might think he's killing you. Remind me not to borrow your cowboy hat.'

'I told Ratso I'd find his mother.'

'But things have turned deadly now,' said McGovern with compassion in his voice. 'Why do you have to be involved personally? Why can't you turn it all over to the cops? Why do you always have to stir things up?'

I puffed patiently on the cigar and thought about why I always had to stir things up. It was a good question. It was also a good cigar.

'The answer is simple,' I told McGovern, 'but the way I feel was described more eloquently by Gustave Flaubert over a hundred years ago. Flaubert said: "I feel very old sometimes. I carry on and would not like to die before having emptied a few more buckets of shit on the heads of my fellow men." '

'Maybe I *will* borrow your cowboy hat,' said McGovern.

74

TWENTY-THREE

*

Keeping information from a woman who wants to know, especially when that woman looks like Stephanie DuPont, is harder than Japanese arithmetic. So, by the time the waiter at the Derby had brought the first bottle of Château de Cat Piss, I was already spilling it, so to speak. Maybe I just wanted to hear myself tell the whole story again to see if there was something I'd missed. I hoped to hell there was, because – short of finding Mary Goodman – there was almost nothing I could do but wait around for the bad guys to realize they'd screwed up and to take another shot at it. 'It' being Ratso or myself.

This, I reflected, was an extremely daunting and dangerous position to be in. Almost as daunting and dangerous as looking across the candlelight at Stephanie DuPont.

'It seems crazy,' said Stephanie, 'to go after the mother after all this time when you could be going after that lawyer. That lawyer sounds suspish. I'm going to law school myself in a couple years, you know.'

'I'll bet I know why you're going to law school,' I said. 'You can't stand the sight of blood.'

'What I can't stand the sight of is that hairball on your lower lip. Get rid of it, Friedman.'

I poured us both another glass of wine and I noticed the waiter standing silently above the table like a well-dressed hovercraft.

'What was that lawyer's name?' asked Stephanie.

'Hamburger.'

'And for the lady?' said the waiter.

'No, no,' I said. 'There's been a terrible misunderstanding. Hamburger's the lawyer who is, no doubt, at this very moment plotting to kill all of us. But before he does I'd like to order two big, hairy steaks. Medium rare okay, Stef?'

'Yes, schmuck-head,' she said, giggling like the schoolgirl that, I suppose, she very nearly was.

'That's Lord Schmuck-head, to you,' I said. Some day I would write a scholarly dissertation comparing why beautiful young girls call middle-aged men disrespectful names with why dogs lick their testicles. Both do it, of course, because they can. If you're the middle-aged man there's nothing you can do but take it in stride and not let it get your goat. Your goat, no doubt, wouldn't want to be disturbed. He's probably very busy licking his testicles.

'Okay,' said Stephanie, 'let's see where we are. Cooperman hasn't called you back and probably still thinks Ratso's dead.'

'That's correct.'

'Ratso's still hiding out in Woodstock so he won't *get* dead.'

'That's correct.'

'And you're sitting on your Hebe ass waiting for your friend Kent Perkins to come to New York and help you find Mary Goodman.'

'That's technically correct. Just like Jesus reportedly told the Mexicans, "Don't do anything until I get back", Kent told me not to poke around looking for Mary Goodman until he gets here. It could create a hot file and alert the wrong people.'

' "Hot file",' she said, laughing. 'I love the way you big private dicks talk.'

'Careful,' I said, 'you may have to eat those words.'

'Friedman,' she said warningly.

It was another facet of the beautiful young girl-middle-aged man scenario. The young girl's language could make a television evangelist blush and it was quite acceptable. The middle-aged man had to be forever on guard against a possible nuance or double entendre that might offend the beautiful young thing's ear. This made, occasionally, for some rather one-sided conversations, but it's been that way since Adam and Eve and Samson and Delilah and it's getting a little late in the game to try to make a rule change now.

'Now just why,' she said, pausing to acknowledge the arrival of the big, hairy steaks, 'do you hold this Kent Perkins in such high regard?'

'Well, for one thing he's a working, licensed private investigator, unlike myself.'

'Who would've guessed?'

'For another, he's an old friend. He's also Ruth Buzzi's husband.'

Stephanie DuPont laughed for a very long time. She laughed so hard there were tears in her eyes. The wine and the candlelight made them look like blue windows in the summer rain.

'What's wrong with being Ruth Buzzi's husband?' I said at last.

'Nothing,' she said. 'It's wonderful. He can stake out the set of Sesame Street.'

'Kent does know a lot about these kinds of investigations. He says you can find anybody if you look hard enough. Claims it's like following a jungle trail and looking for signs – marriages, divorces, illnesses, job changes, voting records, traffic tickets. The skill is in getting strangers to open those records for you. He says he often tells bureaucrats he's a Mormon student checking out his family's genealogy. That way they don't get their antennas up and shut down on him.'

'That's funny,' said Stephanie. 'You don't look like a Mormon student.'

'Kent Perkins says all we need to do is check back to the 1940s and find her date of birth, her social security number, and, if possible, her last known address. With that information he can track her down easily.'

'With that information Pyramus and Thisbe could track her down.'

For a while we both concentrated on the dissection procedures attendant to the meal. As Bob Dylan once said: 'A lot of people got a lot of knives and forks on their tables. They gotta cut something.' It might as well, I figured, be a big, hairy steak. That, very likely, wasn't what Bob had meant, but of course that was always open to interpretation.

'This big, hairy steak is really killer bee,' I said. 'Almost as good as Joe's Jefferson Street Café in Kerrville, Texas.'

'I wouldn't know,' she said.

Possibly, I gazed at Stephanie's eyes a little too long or a little too longingly, but if I did, she didn't seem to notice. Anyway, I like a girl with a good appetite. Evidently, she had one, because it wasn't long before we'd dusted off the big hairies, the waiter'd brought out the dessert menus, and Stephanie was back to badgering me about the investigation.

'So what *are* you going to do until Kent Perkins arrives?'

'I've been thinking a lot about tying a little red bandanna around the cat's neck and taking her out to Central Park to play Frisbee.'

Stephanie snorted a tired, cynical snort. It's extremely difficult for a woman to snort in an attractive fashion, but there was something so primitive in that simple display that it seemed downright sexy. Maybe I was reading too much into it, but she appeared capable of simultaneous sensuality, sophistication, and earthiness and you don't see that every day even in New York. To find those qualities you usually have to look at three different people, and even then, some of them might require a stunt man.

'Okay,' I said, 'I had an idea on the plane coming back from Florida that I might check with some temples and synagogues here in the city. Maybe we can find a Mary Goodman somewhere in their old files.'

'Yeah,' said Stephanie, 'that Mormon missionary shit's really gonna fly big time with some little old rabbi on Long Island.'

'I'll alter the approach slightly,' I said. 'I'll say I'm from the Church of the Latter-Day Businessman.'

Stephanie smiled very briefly and turned her attention to the waiter, who'd materialized again to take our dessert orders.

'How's the cream brûlée?' I asked. The waiter nodded approvingly. Stephanie continued to study her menu.

'You know,' I said, 'I'm somewhat of an expert on cream brûlée. I've ordered it in Houston, I've ordered it in Paris, I've ordered it in Melbourne, Australia. I've even had cream brûlée crossing the Atlantic Ocean on the *QEII*.'

There was a bit of a silence as both Stephanie and the waiter looked at me. Then they looked at each other. Then Stephanie shook her head slightly and gave a small, dry laugh.

'Maybe if you traveled a little further,' she said, 'you'd learn that it's pronounced *crème* brûlée.'

TWENTY-FOUR

*

No one has ever won a waiting game. This was the thought that was in my head when I woke up late the next morning with the cat sleeping on my face and my old Borneo sarong twisted tightly into a rather unpleasant tourniquet around my scrotum. When I'd finally become a homo erectus, fed the cat, made some coffee, lit my first cigar of the morning, and tried to decide whether or not to change the cat litter, it was half past Gary Cooper time and way past time to sit down at my desk and do some cold, deductive, Sherlockian thinking.

I had several crucial executive decisions to make which might have far-reaching repercussions that could impact significantly upon my life, that of my cat, and that of my client in, of course, a random and haphazard order. The cat and the coffee were both sitting on the desk and the smoke from the cigar was filtering upward toward the lesbian dance class, which, I noticed, sounded like it had turned on the juice and cut the damned thing loose. The board meeting was ready to come to order. It was fortunate, I reflected, that I didn't have any stockholders.

According to Anthony Robbins, the California motivational guru, making a decision – any decision – is one of the most important things you can do in your life – eating, sleeping, hosing, dumping, belching, and dying, presumably notwith-standing. Stephanie DuPont, who I once heard refer to Robbins as 'that horse-faced nerd who's sucking everybody dry', also puts great stock in decision-making. The truth is, if you don't make decisions for yourself, one of these days fate will come along and pluck you up by your pretty little neck. Unfortu-nately, if you *do* make decisions, fate will also come along and pluck you up by your pretty little neck. The wisest thing to do is to behave in a decisive manner while assiduously avoiding making any real decisions. That way everyone will respect you enormously until fate comes along and plucks you up by your pretty little neck and everyone claims it was your fault.

'As chief executive,' I said, 'I now bring this meeting to order.'

The cat looked at me with that fabled curiosity almost totally absent from her eyes. The coffee cup continued to send par-ticles of steam toward the ceiling. The cigar also plumed a small bluish-white column ever upward like smoke from a little Mary Poppins chimney. On the rooftop, as fate would have it, were a large group of long-legged young women, many of whom were somewhat confused about their sexuality, and all of whom had fallen under the Sapphic spell of Winnie Katz. They had so little regard for men that they were no doubt oblivious to the fact that one floor below them an important board meeting was taking place.

'Gentlemen,' I said to the cat, who blinked several times rather indignantly, 'today we have a vital decision to make.

There are three possible courses of action, only one of which do we have the time, energy, and manpower to pursue. Each of the three potential courses of action has its own compelling reason for why we should devote our full attention to it. The decision, gentlemen, is up to us.'

I paused here for dramatic effect and gazed purposefully about the boardroom. The cat had gone to sleep on her back with all four paws in the air. The coffee was no longer steaming. The cigar was out. Only the lesbian dance class seemed to maintain its thunder from above, as it probably would for all eternity. Unfazed by any distractions or disappointments, I finished my speech in unfaltering, decisive tones.

'Today, gentlemen, we must decide whether to go after the lawyer, whether to go after Mary Goodman, or whether to change the cat litter.'

At that very moment the phones rang. I picked up the blower on the left.

'Leprosarium for unwed mothers,' I said.

The voice that rasped through the blower belonged to Sergeant Mort Cooperman, and the message it passed along to me was enough to cause anybody's board meeting to adjourn.

Fate, it would seem, had plucked me up by my pretty little neck.

TWENTY-FIVE

*

The late-afternoon sky was gray, and I dodged a few premature snowflakes as I weaved across the Village for my appointment at the cop shop. Cooperman hadn't told me much over the phone but he'd told me enough to make me rather nervous in the service. When I'd told him that Ratso wasn't the victim, he'd launched into a long, knowing, fairly repellent laugh. From the laugh he transitioned to a wheeze, and then he laid the bomb on me. They'd apprehended the killer. Since we were 'colleagues of a sort', and 'in this thing together', he wanted me to come down and meet the perpetrator. I said 'How about sometime later in the week?' and he said 'How about four o'clock?' It was now three forty-seven and I was beginning to feel slightly agitato.

There was a world of things I didn't like and one of them was surprises. As a child, a surprise usually connotes something good. As an adult, the notion of a surprise often indicates you're about to be hosed. I had no idea what Cooperman planned to unveil when I got down to the precinct, but I felt pretty damn sure the surprise wasn't going to be a new pair of skates. Maybe it'd be a load of horseshit, I figured, without the pony.

A sense of personal dread began mounting inside me as I climbed the concrete steps of the precinct house, flicking my cigar at a nearby covey of trash cans. I tried to imagine what Cooperman wanted to show me that he couldn't have told me over the phone. If he'd correctly identified the victim and apprehended the killer, my cowboy hat was off to him, leaving me, of course, with my hair in the shape of the hat, looking like Lyle Lovett's smarter older brother. At the moment, however, I felt decidedly in the debit column in the gray-matter department. What the hell, I thought, it was Cooperman's show and I was merely the invited guest. The only price of admission, it appeared, was a little man inside my gut who kept elbowing me in the colon.

I opened the door and noticed immediately that the desk sergeant had a large red caterpillar crawling extremely slowly across his upper lip. I, for that matter, was in no hurry either. It turned out to be a good thing, because the desk sergeant checked briefly with Cooperman's office and then directed me to a nice cement bench without a park. It was like Cooperman to keep me waiting. It was like Cooperman to gloat over the successful wrap-up of a case. It was not like Cooperman to consider me a 'colleague' or to believe the two of us were 'in this thing together'. The only thing that Cooperman and I were in together was life, and everybody knew that life was just a magazine that had been out of circulation for many years now.

Well, I thought, if Cooperman had indeed caught Jack Bramson's murderer, a lot of the danger to Ratso would certainly be alleviated. As a result, the stress and pressure on myself would be greatly reduced and I might be allowed to go after the lawyer, find Mary Goodman, and empty the cat litter in peace. That's what I was thinking. But things are never what you think.

I was just about nodding out when the desk sergeant nodded me in, and the next thing I knew I was beyond the land of pebbled glass, sitting in front of the cluttered, battle-scarred desk of Sergeant Mort Cooperman. I did not especially like the little smile on his face. He shuffled some papers, shook a cigarette from some off-brand pack, and lit it with his Zippo. I took a fresh cigar out of my hunting vest and began prenuptial arrangements.

'Sorry,' said Sergeant Buddy Fox, as he slunk over from a file cabinet. 'No pipes or cigars.'

'The victim,' said Cooperman, 'as we learned almost immediately from the lab, was not your pal. It turned out to be a friend of his. Guy name of Jack Bramson. Lived in Queens. Looked out for the place sometimes when your pal left town for the weekend. This time, apparently, he didn't look out too good.'

'Tell me something I don't know, Sergeant.' Cooperman's smile became slightly broader, and if possible, slightly more unpleasant.

'If you're still clinging to your conspiracy theory connection of this guy getting whacked having something to do with your brilliant adoption investigation, you can forget it. We got the killer. We overheard his confession. And we got him confessing on tape.'

At this point Cooperman stood up abruptly and signaled like a traffic cop for me to follow him.

'Teatime's over,' said Fox.

Cooperman led the way down a narrow corridor past more offices, more pebbled glass, ringing telephones, muffled voices redolent with the trivia and the tragedy of the big city. It was a hallway like any other except that it held a strange, jangly sort of ambience not dissimilar to that of an emergency corridor in a big-city hospital. As you walked by you could almost feel the cool, sweet downdraft from the fateful flutter of the wings of life and death.

We descended a small flight of stairs with Cooperman in front, myself in the middle, and Fox bringing up the rear. It felt like being sandwiched between two relentless walking book-ends. Several uniforms were moving about the hallway when we reached the next floor down. One walked close by us on the right. Cooperman acknowledged him with all the regard one might have for a passing dragonfly. Clearly, the detective sergeant was a man on a mission. He motioned to a guard and a large iron-barred door swung open ahead of us. We walked through it into a cool, dank, tomb-like place where Cooperman finally stopped and turned around.

'I think I told you,' he said, 'that once we caught the killer you'd see that the whole thing was pretty simple and close to home. You remember me saying that, Tex?'

I nodded. I remembered.

'Well, it did turn out to be pretty simple. And if you'll direct your attention over to that holding cell you'll see that it turned out to be about as close to home as you can get.'

I looked where Cooperman was pointing and I vaguely made out a solitary figure huddled in the corner of the cell. I walked a few steps closer and squinted my eyes to see more clearly through the gloom. But what I saw only managed to increase the gloom I felt in my heart.

It was Ratso.

TWENTY-SIX
*

Robert Louis Stevenson was once asked to contribute a short story for a religious tract that was being circulated in Samoa by a local missionary friend. The story that Stevenson wrote for the little magazine was known as 'The Bottle Imp' and before long became a world classic. It is the tale of a man who comes into ownership, at a very low price, of a magic imp in a bottle who will grant him any material wish he desires. The imp originally came into the world through a deal with the devil and, so the story goes, any man who dies with the imp in his possession will go to hell. Although the price of the imp is only a few cents, no one is foolish enough to purchase it, because the resale prospects are fairly hideous, along with, of course, the prospects of what happens to you if you fall through the trapdoor with the imp as part of your estate.

The man is in a frenzy to get rid of the imp but can find no buyers, so he tries to give it away. When he returns home, like magic, there is the imp again. The man leaves the bottle on a park bench, throws it into the sea, possibly endeavors to recycle it as well, all to no avail. The imp in the bottle always returns somehow to its doomed and desperate master. It will grant him any wish in the world with the sole exception of health, happiness, and peace of mind.

The natives of Samoa, having been the first in the world to have read the story, became convinced, quite understandably, that it was not a work of fiction. They had observed firsthand their beloved friend's unaccountable moods of melancholia in paradise. They had observed his fragile, gentle nature, seen his health deteriorate to the point of death. They wondered openly how a man who appeared to have so much could be so achingly lonesome for his friends, his childhood, his home in Scotland, his own culture, and everything else that people who have everything have always longed for. The natives of Samoa came to believe that in a secret safe somewhere in his great plantation house Robert Louis Stevenson had locked away the bottle imp.

I had to admit, as I looked at Ratso, that try as I might, it sometimes seemed I could never get rid of him. He did have a singular propensity for popping up in my life in moments and places that always brought me aggravation and grief. Now, as Cooperman graciously opened the cell door to allow me a few minutes with the prisoner, I noticed that Ratso's eyes and the features of his face had vaguely come to resemble my mental image of the imp in the bottle.

If Ratso's appearance, not to mention his mere presence in the cell, had seemed distressing, the halting, one-way attempt at conversation with him was even more troubling. When he'd called me two days earlier from Woodstock he'd sounded like his normal, ebullient, bordering-on-tedious self. Now, he looked and acted like a man whose whole world had suddenly been kicked out from under him.

There was an absence of warmth and almost an absence of recognition in his eyes when I went over to him in the corner of the cell. When I asked him how he'd happened to have gotten here, he just despondently put his head in his hands. Obviously, he hadn't followed my instructions to stay in Woodstock, but this was hardly the time or place to mention it. When I asked more questions, Ratso behaved in an almost childlike, next door to autistic, manner, either shaking his head or turning away into the corner. About the only thing he said that seemed remotely intelligible was when I asked him, incredulously, if he'd actually killed Bramson.

'Hausenfluck,' he said. 'Talk to Hausenfluck.'

Ratso had mentioned Hausenfluck to me in passing during earlier conversations. He was Ratso's downstairs neighbor, an elderly man, a former schoolteacher, who, if I remembered correctly, had fairly recently been experiencing certain emotional problems largely associated with the bottle. I, too, I thought, had been recently experiencing certain emotional problems largely associated with the bottle. The only difference between Hausenfluck's situation and mine was that my bottle appeared to contain an imp.

It didn't look like I was going to get any more out of Ratso, and Cooperman was making not-so-subtle departure gestures in the doorway of the cell, so I gripped Ratso's arm and left him with the one-word advice Sancho Panza occasionally gave Don Quixote when the situation looked hopeless: 'Courage!'

Out in the hallway again I assured Cooperman that he was holding the wrong man. Regardless of Ratso's apparent state of clinical depression, it was against his very nature to have committed the crime. Cooperman took my objections in stride and calmly explained that Ratso had come back to the city early that morning, crossed the crime scene ribbons illegally, entered his own apartment, and, when his neighbor, a man named Hausenfluck, had called him, admitted he'd killed Jack Bramson. Since Ratso had picked up the phone after the message tape was rolling, the confession had been recorded on his own machine, the tape now residing in the hands of the police.

Ratso had been in custody only a few hours, but almost surely would not be offered bail because in his current mental state he was certainly a flight risk. A doctor was on the way to examine him. A formal interview was also soon to be conducted by Cooperman. But Ratso had already repeated to police what he'd told Hausenfluck on the tape: 'I killed Jack Bramson.'

'He didn't kill Jack Bramson,' I said, as we walked back up the stairs to the first floor.

'Better tell him that,' said Fox.

There was a dull throbbing in my head that caused me to have to concentrate on thinking clearly. I knew Ratso was innocent. He must've just been overwhelmed by a sudden remorse after I'd spoken to him about the loss of his friend. He'd blamed himself for Bramson's death, a quite natural thing for a close friend to do, and New York's finest had taken him literally at his word, a quite natural thing for them to do.

'Look,' said Cooperman. 'Don't you worry about him, Tex. He's in good hands. I'm gonna be interviewing him myself. A doctor's on his way. He's already called a lawyer. There's nothing you can do.'

'Who's the lawyer?' I said.

'Who'd he call, Fox?' said Cooperman. 'Funny-sounding name, wasn't it?'

'Yeah,' said Fox. 'He could've been confused. Could've thought he was ordering dinner.'

I turned to Fox impatiently, but he'd already stepped into the doorway of a little room to talk to a woman who looked like an aging prostitute. I was beginning to feel like an aging prostitute myself. I walked over to the doorway and stood there until Fox and the woman looked up.

'Can I help you, Tex?'

'Yes, Sergeant. What was that lawyer's name?'

'Hamburger,' he said.

TWENTY-SEVEN

When I left the cop shop, I did not return to the loft. The loft, I figured, was in good hands. With the cat in charge, and Sherlock, the cockroaches, and the answering machine to help out, there was almost no foreseeable situation they couldn't deal with. If something came up they couldn't handle, it wouldn't get handled. Right now I had work to do. Ratso was clearly out where the buses don't run, and if I didn't find some answers quick his ass was going to belong to the gypsies. For one who had so recently come back from the dead only to arrive at a fate worse than death, he seemed to be holding up about as well as could be expected. That was more than I could say for myself.

The snowflakes had increased in number now, and as I rambled down through Sheridan Square they wandered through the sky in all directions like yesterday's brain cells. I didn't know exactly what to do. I just knew that whatever it was, I'd better do it fast and right.

I was obviously heading somewhere, but I wasn't really thinking about it. All kinds of unbidden images from the past kept unreeling themselves in the old closed-for-the-winter drive-in theater of my brain. I saw myself, Ratso, and Mike Simmons down the street in the Monkey's Paw together on an evening just like this one many lunar landings ago. Simmons was a very bright, decent guy with a good heart and the only blemish on our relationship was that he'd hosed my last five former girlfriends before they'd had a chance to become former girlfriends.

Maybe it was, as Ratso had said, a form of latent homosexual flattery, or maybe Simmons just liked my taste in women and was too lazy to go and find them for himself, or maybe it had something to do with the fact that back then there was more marching powder around than snowflakes, but I never really got mad at Michael until the day I caught him eyeing the cat.

'Why're you looking at her that way?'

'She's beautiful. So graceful.'

'Don't get any ideas.'

'What the hell are you talking about?'

'I don't want you hosin' that cat.'

'I'd never hose your cat. It's the only meaningful female relationship you've ever had.'

And he kept his word.

For some reason, Simmons's persistent involvement in my love affairs never seemed to get up my sleeve. For one thing, he was always a gentleman about it. He even once suggested that I point out women to him that I was attracted to so he would then be able to hose them *before* I became involved with them. In this way, he averred, he would provide sort of a one-man protective health service for me in this modern era of AIDS and other sexually transmitted diseases. I mulled over the offer.

Unfortunately, Simmons left for California shortly after that and, ever since, my relationships with women seem to linger on just a little longer than either party desires, languishing, atrophying, rotting away until even friendship follows love out the door and leaves nothing behind but an old pair of red cowboy boots and a cup of blue coffee.

I stopped at a corner and jotted down Simmons's name in my little notebook. There'd been reports that he was back in town. If I could find him maybe he'd intercede in my relationship with Ratso. If Ratso got bail, Simmons could hold his hand, baby-sit him, and keep him out of further trouble, though I couldn't imagine how much deeper he could possibly dig himself. Or if Ratso stayed in jail, which now appeared likely, Simmons could bring him bologna sandwiches and lots of books about Hitler, Jesus, and Bob Dylan. Either way, Simmons could take Ratso off my hands psychologically and leave me free to pursue what was now becoming an investigation of a somewhat more desperate nature. If I couldn't find another good candidate for Jack Bramson's murderer, Ratso might very well be smoke.

As I crossed Seventh Avenue against the light, the way everybody does in New York and Paris and nobody does in Germany or Beverly Hills, I still strongly clung to the notion that if I could learn who actually killed Bramson, the secrets of Ratso's adoption would also be revealed. Bramson's death and the search for Ratso's mother were so intimately connected in my mind that not even Mike Simmons could put a wedge between them, provided, of course, that I could locate Mike Simmons. Of late, I seemed to be better at losing people than finding them, a trait that could, on occasion, prolong your life and could also, on occasion, make you wonder why you bothered.

The night was dark and cold and the snow was still falling as I trudged past a gay bar I'd once visited during the course of a murder investigation that McGovern had gotten himself mixed up in. I remembered walking into the place, sitting down at the bar, and ordering a drink. Then a guy had come up behind me and had given me the oldest gay pickup line in the world: 'Can I push in your stool for you?'

There was no question, I thought, that the Village derived much of its unique flavor from the gays, artists, and weirdos who lived there, along with, of course, the worker bees, serial killers, propeller-heads, bean counters, Reform rabbis, and pet shrinks who pretty much comprised the normal population. It was a bit disconcerting, when I stopped to think about it, that I seemed to fit into the milieu. Tonight, however, I sure as hell didn't want to stop and think about it. There'd be time for that when I found Mary Goodman.

As I crossed Sixth Avenue into SoHo, past all the trendy stores that sold stuff nobody needed, I shook all errant thoughts and snowflakes from my head. I ankled it up West Broadway and took a right on Prince Street, where I stopped in front of a familiar building that now appeared as spooky-looking as the artwork of a troubled child. The troubled child who usually lived here, I was well aware, had recently been incommoded and relocated to the sneezer.

I didn't know why Ratso hadn't told me about McLane, the now-deceased private dick he'd first hired to find his mother. I almost didn't want to know why the hell Ratso had tried to make a jailhouse call to Hamburger the lawyer. All I knew was that Ratso didn't live here anymore.

So I unfurled my butterfly net and pushed Hausenfluck's buzzer.

TWENTY-EIGHT

*

'Am I being rude, mother?' asked Cecil Hausenfluck in a highly agitato, near-hysterical falsetto voice.

'Is your mother in the bedroom?' I said.

'This is a studio apartment,' said Hausenfluck.

'I see.'

So there was no bedroom and there was no mother, unless, of course, she'd come back to haunt Hausenfluck in the form of the large tasseled floor lamp he'd appeared to direct his question to. God knows there were enough other things haunting the man. Why not his mother disguised as an antique floor lamp? At least he could turn her off occasionally.

'So, earlier this morning you made a telephone call to Ratso,' I said.

'Earlier this morning I made a telephone call to Ratso,' he stated, mimicking my intonation precisely.

'Why did you call him?'

'I wanted to tell him about the little children coming back and the Big Bad Wolf at the door.'

'I see,' I said again, but, of course, I didn't. No one ever really saw the things that the Cecil Hausenflucks of the world did. Well, maybe Anne Frank, Joan of Arc, and Van Gogh saw those things, but look what happened to them. They all died inconceivably hideous deaths and now they live with God, who, judging from the state of the planet these days, doesn't see too damn well Himself. Maybe Texas State Optical's got something for Him.

'Maybe this isn't a good time,' I said, as Hausenfluck began trying to establish eye contact with a half-eaten turkey drumstick on the table. 'Maybe I should come back another time and let you finish your meal.'

'I've eaten an appropriate amount for my figure,' he said, in a prim, take-no-prisoners falsetto.

'Fine,' I said. 'Let's get back to your conversation with Ratso.'

'He's a fine young man, isn't he?'

'He certainly is.'

'Well, you know, he helps me sometimes when the little children come and play tricks on me. They're little tricksters, they are. Hide my money sometimes. Last week they hid my reading glasses. Haven't found them yet.'

'What do they look like?' I said. 'These little children.'

With his right foot, Hausenfluck almost synaptically kicked his left ankle twice. It was a small thing but nonetheless rather disconcerting to the casual visitor. When he spoke, there was a total absence of guile in his features. Clearly, he believed every word he said.

'The little children have little faces and little heads just like little children but they're not little children. They're really very evil, demonic creatures. They have little, short bodies. No legs. No arms. Am I being rude, mother?'

His mother didn't answer.

Neither did I.

He was watching my face carefully now for any trace of doubt or skepticism. I shook my head slightly in a sympathetic manner and strived to achieve the vapid, expressionless countenance you affect when you know that a well-respected child molester's about to feed you a communion wafer.

'About a month ago,' Hausenfluck continued, 'I had to move all my furniture out into the hall there by the elevator just to keep them from hiding behind things. Ratso helped me move that heavy desk there into the hallway. He's a fine young fellow, isn't he?'

'He certainly is.'

'Don't know what I'd do without him.'

You're about to find out, I thought. I'd had about enough of the little children and I figured it might be time to steer things on to the Big Bad Wolf at the door and then follow that by walking out the door myself. This guy was cookin' on a planet that hadn't even been discovered yet.

'So tell me about the Big Bad Wolf at your door,' I said, as I blithely watched him kick himself twice in the ankle again. It was a painful thing to watch, but it seemed to get him on track. Maybe I'd try it myself, I thought, if I ever got home from the third ring of Saturn.

'Not *my* door,' he was saying.

'What?'

'The Big Bad Wolf was at Ratso's door.'

Hausenfluck was smiling a little smile and humming to himself now. He wasn't going to make a great government witness or anything, but he was all I had going for me at the time. I had to keep him focused on the Big Bad Wolf.

'When did you see the Big Bad Wolf?'

'Let me see. It was three nights ago, I think. Yes, that's right, because I needed Ratso's help to move all my clothes into the hallway because the little children were hiding in the closet. Did I tell you about the little children?'

'You mentioned them in passing. What did the Big Bad Wolf do?'

'He was knock, knock, knockin' on Ratso's door, just like that Bob Dylan song Ratso's always playing. Then he huffed and he puffed and he blew the door down and I got scared and I got back on the elevator and came back here and one of the little children had taken my keys and I had to wake up the super so he could let me back in.'

'But you saw the Big Bad Wolf?'

'Of course.'

'Describe him to me.'

'Well, he – GET OFF THE DRAPES!! YOU'LL RIP THE FUCKING DRAPES!!! STOP HANGING ON THE FUCKING DRAPES!!! I'M GONNA GET THE BROOM!! WHERE'D YOU HIDE THE FUCKING BROOM?!! – '

Hausenfluck was screaming now at the top of his lungs. He jumped up as if something had bitten him, violently knocking over the coffee table and sending the half-eaten turkey leg on a nice little trajectory over the floor lamp. I took a few steps forward to calm him down but he leapt across the room like a leprechaun on cruise control.

'THERE'S ONE ON THE COUCH!! HE WAS SITTING RIGHT NEXT TO ME!! GET THEM OUT OF HERE!! GET THEM OUT OF HERE!!!'

I didn't know whether to shake Hausenfluck like a rag doll or throw water on him or just try to help him get the little children out of there. I finally opted for going into the kitchen and looking for some brandy. I banged around for a while with Hausenfluck screaming in the background and every time I opened a cabinet, about eight hundred empty liquor bottles fell out on top of me which, I reasoned, could've been a contributing factor to Hausenfluck's dementia.

Eventually, I found a nearly full bottle of brandy and poured us both a healthy glass; neither of us needed much coaxing to pour it down our necks. Hausenfluck wanted to dance again and I didn't want him to drink alone so I gave us both a very generous second round. A short time later, with Cecil

Hausenfluck snoring quietly on the couch, I let myself out. I closed the door softly and left him there with his little children.

I took the sad, small elevator down to the lobby and walked out of Ratso's building and went down to the corner to look for a taxi. It had stopped snowing and the night air had sort of a cold, crystalline, Zhivago-like comfort about it.

'Am I being rude, mother?' I said to the New York sky.

My mother didn't answer either.

TWENTY-NINE
*

Kent Perkins blew into town the next morning like a large, blond California condor and he hit the ground flapping. He wanted first of all for the two of us to take a working Los Angeles power brunch during which I was to report to him the details of the case from start to finish.

'I'll tell you everything I can remember,' I said, 'but I'm not Archie Goodwin.'

'Who's Archie Goodwin?' he said.

'A fictional detective.'

'Every good detective is a fictional detective,' said Perkins. 'It's not an exact science. The guys with all the answers, the hard-asses and headline grabbers, they rarely get the job done. The best PI work is usually performed by people who seem almost not to exist.'

It was a pretty insightful observation, I thought, for a guy who'd never heard of Archie Goodwin. Of course, you couldn't blame him. Nero Wolfe was a large, sedentary, cerebral, middle-aged, fat man who almost never got into a car, much less a car chase. In order to portray him in a movie, someone like Tom Hanks would have to bulk up to about four hundred pounds and even then the opportunities to emote would be severely restricted to the pushing out and pulling in of one's lips just prior to the solution of the case. For these reasons, Nero Wolfe had never made it to the movies, and people in Hollywood, who seldom if ever read books, would have no way of knowing that his sidekick was Archie Goodwin. To be totally fair, it is also unlikely that Archie Goodwin had ever heard of Tom Hanks.

For the first time in a long while I was starting to feel a little better about the way the investigation was going. I'd been able to reach Mike Simmons the night before and he seemed very eager to step in for me and spend some quality time with Ratso. Not that Ratso was going anywhere, but I figured that between Simmons and the NYPD he'd be kept safely on ice long enough for Perkins and myself to come up with another candidate for Rikers Island.

Besides, there was something about Kent Perkins, other than his being large and blond and from California, that inspired confidence, or at least a measure of trust. He was pleasant, modest, and engaging, which was more than I could say for most of my New York friends, and though he was a private investigator, he seemed to have a profound respect for the law. This differed markedly from Rambam's approach, which was that the law was an ass and needed to be kicked periodically with a pointy-toed cowboy boot. That was probably one of the reasons why Rambam was wanted in every state that started with an 'I'.

I took Kent Perkins to Big Wong's restaurant in Chinatown for our power brunch. As we entered the place, the cooks and waiters all lined up behind the counter and shouted in unison: 'Oooh-lah-lah! Oooh-lah-lah! Kee-kee! Chee-chee! Kee-kee! Chee-chee!'

I oooh-lah-lahed back a few times and took the reception

smoothly and graciously in the manner of Frank Sinatra entering some small café in Little Italy.

Kent Perkins was duly impressed.

The manager, who stood behind the Jewish piano and spoke very little English, nodded about seven times to me and Kent and then looked around.

'Where Raz-zo?' he said.

'Don't ask,' I told him.

The 'kee-kee, chee-chee' greeting for Ratso and myself was a tradition at Big Wong's that seldom had varied over the years, Ratso and I having very possibly frequented the place more than any man, woman, or child on the planet. The precise meaning of the words 'kee-kee, chee-chee' is open to some debate. Ratso and I have always considered them to be terms of endearment and have acted accordingly, considering the Big Wong waiters, despite the fact that few spoke English, to be some of our most loyal, reliable friends in the city. Sometimes they were our only friends in the city.

Ted Mann, the former editor of *National Lampoon* and a writer for *NYPD Blue*, is an old pal of mine and has a slightly different interpretation of the 'kee-kee, chee-chee' greeting. It is Ted's contention, and he claims he has researched the matter, that these two words are not really terms of endearment. He believes that 'kee-kee' and 'chee-chee' are actual Mandarin words that mean 'crazy' and 'smelly', respectively. Ted suspects, as well, that the Chinese waiters think of Ratso and myself as a pair of friendly, rather eccentric, homosexuals because we come in together so often and never with a woman.

Kent and I were shown to a special table in the back room and by the time we'd finished the first course of wonton mein soup I'd regurgitated upon him everything there was to know about the search for Mary Goodman. Kent made a few notes in a little notebook as I yapped, and I was heartened to observe that his pages flipped over the top of the pad like a cop's rather than to the side, like a poetry major or a cub reporter for the *Daily Planet*.

'Okay, Kink,' said Kent Perkins, 'let's start with the license number for the two good ol' boys with the assault rifle who followed you to the airport in Miami. Then we can move on to the roast pork. I love roast pork.'

'It speaks very highly of you,' I said, as I looked over my Big Chief tablet, found the license number, and recited it to Kent, who jotted it down in his little notebook and flipped another page.

During the next hour or so Perkins made more abrupt trips to the pay phone than a bookie with Tourette's syndrome. He was the only large, Aryan-looking person in the place which added a rather humorous component to the process, especially when the waiters came to our table, pointed to the front of the restaurant, then pointed at Kent and said, 'You!'

As Kent explained it, he had a friend who was a detective on the Miami police force and another contact with the Florida Department of Motor Vehicles, and he hoped to learn who owned or had leased the car before the fortune cookies arrived.

'We may be waiting a long time,' I said. 'Look around. No honkies. No fortune cookies.'

But Kent Perkins was already up answering the pay phone, jotting information in his little notebook, and staring lustfully at the large pieces of roast pork hanging behind the glass counter and dripping grease onto the chopping board. While Kent was otherwise disposed, I ordered him a large portion of roast pork. I also ordered spare ribs with black bean sauce, soya sauce chicken chopped with the bone and ginger sauce on the side, and a big helping of bok choy with oyster sauce, most of which was already navigating my lower intestine before Perkins had had a chance to touch the roast pork.

'Don't wait for me,' I said, as Perkins again returned to the table, 'go right ahead.'

'The car,' said Perkins with a big Texas smile, 'was leased by

99

the Bimini Corporation. They're right here in little ol' New York. I've got the address and the suite number.'

'What do we do now?'

'First, I'm gonna finish this meal. As soon as I do that, we're gonna find the guy who rented that car and I'm gonna kick his ass.'

'You are?' I said, puffing speculatively on my cigar.

'That's right,' said Kent Perkins. 'And it don't take me long to eat roast pork.'

THIRTY

*

Kent Perkins was right. It didn't take him long to eat roast pork. What did take up a large portion of our adult lives was finding a cab in Chinatown. This, however, was not necessarily time poorly spent, for it gave me a chance to observe Kent, and it gave Kent a chance to observe New York, which he professed to be enjoying very much in spite of the fact that it was cold and rainy and every store we passed sold buddhas, Chinese parasols, and Chicago Bulls caps.

We stopped at one restaurant window filled with giant vermilion squids hanging next to rows of ducks with hooks in what used to be their eyeballs. There was also a whole pig hanging upside down with sightless eye sockets that seemed to say: 'I am the reincarnation of Mussolini.'

'Almost makes you want to be a vegetarian,' I said.

'Either that,' said Perkins, 'or corner the market on pork-belly futures.'

'What I'd really like to corner is the Bimini Corporation.'

'The fact that they rented the car that tried to whack you in Florida is very damning information.'

'I know,' I said, 'but it's not going to be easy for you to kick a whole corporation's ass.'

'I've come up against corporations before,' said Kent, as he bundled up against the cold. 'These old boys are probably slicker than owl shit on a pump handle, but when we find that head honcho I'm gonna hit him so hard his polo shirt's gonna roll up his spine like a venetian blind.'

'That's good,' I said. 'We never have any excitement here in New York.'

'We're fixin' to,' said Kent. 'This could get even more exciting than the time in L.A. when you generated that enormous toxic gas expulsion inside the tobacco humidor.'

'You sure that was me?'

There was not even a nuance of a cab anywhere along Mott Street. We walked in a light rain a little further up the block and I again reflected on the Kris Kristofferson 'walking contradiction' that was Kent Perkins. Under a macho, Texas, barnyard humoresque façade there stood an extremely intelligent, deeply sensitive American with a sense of loyalty and dedication that were becoming increasingly hard to find in the country of his birth. What he set out to do, he almost always accomplished. At that moment I came close to feeling a twinge of sympathy for whoever was standing in the well-polished, wing-tipped wheels of the CEO of the Bimini Corporation.

'By the way,' said Kent, 'when we get to this address and suite number, don't expect it to be the actual office suites of the Bimini Corporation.'

'Long as it's not a window with a pig in it, I'd call it progress.'

'All I'm saying is that if they're capable enough and big enough and bad enough to come within a Mickey Mouse whisker of sending you to Disney World forever, they're also smart enough not to have their actual headquarters at the address we're headed to. That is if we ever find a cab. C'mon, Kink, tell me the truth. Are there really taxicabs in New York?'

'Yes, Virginia, there are. They've just never heard of a man from Los Angeles walking and they're enjoying the novelty of it.'

We continued walking down the winding end of Mott Street, then turned around and retraced our steps back up toward Canal. Looking for a cab can sometimes be a zen, not to say tedious, experience. If you look too hard in too many places you'll never find one. It's often better to go to the place where you started and just wait.

'There's one thing we've got in our favor,' said Perkins, as the two of us stood under a metal awning outside the place where the pig was hanging.

'We're both Jewish?'

'Afraid not, Kink. The Spoiler's never seen a knife.'

'You could always borrow the one in my back,' I said, as I cut the butt off a new cigar, only vaguely aware of the Freudian implications of my actions.

'What I'm saying,' said Kent, in that way he had of being suddenly serious, 'is that we have a window of opportunity to work with and we should take advantage of it. At the very least, these guys believe that Ratso is dead, because they're under the impression they killed him themselves. If they're really clever, they already know they got the wrong guy and that Ratso's been arrested for the murder. Either way, they should be off their guard for a while now, and that may be all the window we need to get the drop on them.'

After that, things happened rather quickly. I lit a cigar, and, as I looked up, saw a guy getting out of a taxi just across the street.

'There's a cab,' I shouted, and both of us moved toward it like we'd been shot out of a circus cannon.

About half a nanosecond later the circus cannon returned a volley in our direction, right at the empty spot where the two of us had been standing under the awning. I turned around and saw a squid splinter into a million pieces, the pig suddenly spinning like a dreidel, and the window shattering into shiny icicles of glass.

Perkins had a gun out and was crouching behind a parked car scouring the street. I'd found the narrow sanctuary of a pay-phone booth with a little Chinese pagoda on top of it. For a moment time seemed to hang there like a dead pig. Then people began pouring out of the restaurant where, amazingly, no one had been hurt. Cars continued to drive slowly by in the rain. The rain continued to fall on the sidewalk. The sidewalk lay there like the old whore that it was, resplendent in the rain with bright shards of broken glass reflecting off it like costume jewelry.

'So much for our window of opportunity,' I said.

THIRTY-ONE
*

'Well, fuck me naked runnin' backwards on a tractor,' said Kent Perkins, as he glared angrily out the window of the taxi.

'I'm just happy,' I said, 'to get out of Chinatown without an acupuncture treatment.'

'It doesn't change anything,' said Kent. 'It just means we'd better be careful as a pair of porcupine pickers with the palsy.'

Kent had taken the cab driver through a series of sharp, unexpected turns, U-turns, and figure eights for the past twenty minutes and, as far as I was concerned, any possible pursuer who was still with us was welcome to hop in the cab and go along for the ride. That included my stomach.

I was moderately impressed with Perkins's diversionary tactics, especially considering that the only person in New York who appeared to know the city less well than Kent Perkins was our Cambodian cab driver. Of course, getting lost in a city deliberately is not always as easy as it looks. Lots of people get lost in lots of cities every day of the year, but, like belching or farting, only a chosen few can do it on command.

It was a funny old world, I thought, as I watched Kent leaning over the front seat to help the Cambodian navigate the mean streets of New York. The big, friendly Texan was, by any reckoning, at least three times the size of the tiny little Cambodian, yet the Cambodian had probably seen ten times the amount of shit in his life and I wasn't referring to horseshit or cow shit but to human misery, which often takes a lot longer to scrape off your boots.

A short while later, midtown on Lex, we spotted the building that the Bimini Corporation, whatever or whoever that was, had given as the address for its home office. Kent told the driver to go past it and drive around the block.

'What do you suppose the Bimini Corporation actually does?' I said. 'Other than shoot out windows in Chinatown.'

'We're about to find out,' said Kent, as he signaled the driver to pull over a good city block away from the building.

As Kent Perkins strode purposefully up the street toward the address in question, the cab driver, who must've come from western Cambodia, turned on a country music station. I immediately heard Garth Brooks. The anti-Hank. I puffed on my cigar and half-listened to Garth Brooks the way everybody does to country music these days and mourned the passing of the undecaffeinated era of the fifties and sixties. I missed Hank Williams and Johnny Horton, who both died young, tragic, perfectly timed country-music deaths, and who'd both, incidentally, been married to Billie Jean Horton. Captain Midnite, my friend in Nashville, always contended that Billie Jean had been some sort of a witch and that she'd killed Hank Williams and Johnny Horton and stunted Faron Young's growth.

My growth, unfortunately, was being stunted as well. My growth was being stunted by Ratso. When I'd first told him I'd help him find his real mother I hadn't envisaged the project becoming my life's work. Now the search had grown not only tedious but dangerous. Jack Bramson was dead, Ratso was in the sneezer, and whoever wanted to wax me in Florida was still trying to polish me off in New York.

Nevertheless, I had great confidence in Kent Perkins. Though he didn't know New York very well, he'd had great success with this line of work all through the West. He had a way with people. He was the quintessential good cop. And I trusted his instinct that getting to the bottom of the Bimini Corporation might be the fastest way to find out what had happened to Mary Goodman.

Moments later, Perkins came back to the cab and leaned his large head in the window. The look on his face was not encouraging.

'It's just a small mail drop,' he said. 'Just rows and rows of boxes and a three-hundred-pound black woman in charge who's mean as a snake.'

'Doesn't look too promising.'

'Just give me a while. Remember, I'm very good with people.'

'You're not doing too well with me.'

'Look, give me a couple of hours. Just take the cab home and I'll call you at your place. Don't you have something to do around the house? Vacuum the den or something?'

'I don't have a den and the only vacuum I seem to be experiencing is the continued absence of information about the Bimini Corporation.'

'You'll soon know more than you ever wanted to.'

'Fine. If I never hear from you again, I'll assume you're either dead or you're just a California guy who doesn't always get back in touch when he says he will.'

'I'll call you in two hours.'

'I'll change the cat litter.'

Perkins was better than his word. I'd been back at the loft only a little over an hour when the telephone rang. As a creature of narrow habit, I answered the blower on the left.

'Bimini Corporation,' I said.

'Not according to my information,' said Perkins. 'Whatever in the blue-eyed buck-naked hell is goin' on around here, at least now we know where to find it.'

'Okay,' I said. 'Spit it.'

'The real office of Bimini Corporation is over on the West Side. I've got the address and I'm headed there now. I'm just going to look it over. I'm not going in. I think we should do that tonight. Late tonight.'

'How'd you get the address?'

'You wouldn't believe me if I told you. There's a cab. Got to go. I'll call you back.'

There wasn't a hell of a lot for me to do except change the cat litter.

So I did.

THIRTY-TWO

*

It was getting dark and I still hadn't heard again from Kent Perkins. I stood at the kitchen window of the loft, smoking a cigar, drinking a cup of black coffee, and watching the night creep its way across Vandam Street. I'd tried to make myself useful that afternoon by calling Moie Hamburger's office, Cooperman, Ratso in jail, and Michael Simmons. I'd gone 0-for-four. Hamburger was still gone, Cooperman was out, Ratso was in, of course, but couldn't take the call, and Simmons was 'no longer staying here' according to the rather testy young woman who'd answered the phone. I asked if she had a number for him and she said: 'Let your fingers do the walking.'

If Kent and I couldn't get somewhere with the trail of the Bimini Corporation, I had damn few cards left to play. I could coax McGovern into doing a piece for the paper about Ratso's search for his mother, but what they used to call human interest didn't hold people's interest these days. I could call a lawyer friend of mine in California, Phil Kaplan, and see if he had any hot ideas about finding Hamburger, but getting a lawyer to find a lawyer might get complicated. I could wear a sandwich board advertising for Mary Goodman and walk around the Village but most people would probably think it was performance art. I could call the local temples and synagogues posing as a Mormon missionary. That might bring interesting results. Or I could simply deal myself out, which, as the night and the light and the half-light grew darker still, I came very close to doing.

The same case that seemed to have been all but wrapped up in Florida a scant few days ago now appeared to be cracking and falling apart like the sidewalks of New York. In a mood of near-desperation, I sat down at the desk, picked up the blower, and called Phil Kaplan, the lawyer in California.

'Argue, Pearson, Harbison, & Myers,' said Margo, the receptionist with whom I often chatted while waiting for Phil.

'Any law firm that begins with Argue can't be all bad,' I said.

'Kinky!' she said enthusiastically. Some women liked the name Kinky and some didn't, and whether they were kinky or not didn't seem to have a lot to do with it. Margo just liked the name Kinky. We'd never met and that was probably a good thing.

When Phil came on the line I explained briefly what a Moie Hamburger was and why I wanted to find one. Phil sounded surprisingly optimistic about things. All people in California sound surprisingly optimistic about things.

'There's a book,' said Phil, 'called Martindale-Hubble. It's a directory of lawyers and it gives information that might very well help us find this guy.'

'I know he exists,' I said. 'I've met him once.'

'We'll find him,' said Phil, growing more confident. All people in California grow more confident the longer they talk to you. That's why most Americans keep their West Coast calls rather brief.

Phil said he'd check it out that night and get back to me tomorrow. I told him fine and thanked him.

'May all your juries be well hung,' I said, as I cradled the blower and took a fresh cigar out of Sherlock Holmes's head.

'You know,' I said to the cat, 'it makes sense that Kent would pursue the fresher trail of last week's license plate rather than try to find a woman who hasn't bothered to see her son in forty-seven years. Either she's dead or she doesn't give a damn.'

The cat sat on the desk and looked at me.

'Of course that could apply to a lot of people we haven't heard from.'

I struck a kitchen match and lit the cigar, rotating it slowly, holding it ever so slightly above the level of the flame, and watching two bright candles in the eyes of the cat as they burned away another moment of the obsidian night.

I'd just taken a puff when the phones rang. I exhaled and collared the blower on the left.

It was Kent Perkins, and he wanted me to meet him at a little coffee shop at midnight somewhere in Hell's Kitchen. He also wanted me to bring a long pole, like a fishing pole, and to wear a cowboy hat.

'Is this a scavenger hunt or a fishing expedition?' I said. 'I need to know how to dress.'

'Kink, we're going into a private underground parking garage. There's an infra-red light beam controlling the gate. I've got a lot to do between now and midnight. Just wear your hat and bring about a six-foot pole of some kind.'

'Have you thought of using the spoiler?'

'That's only for big hook-and-ladder jobs. And by the way, this is sort of a fishing expedition. You know what my dad in Texas used to tell me when I was a kid?'

'Don't tell mom I'm hosin' the baby-sitter?'

'Kink,' said Kent chidingly. 'My dad said: "Always fish where the big fish swim." '

'We'd better catch a big one fast,' I said. 'I don't plan on hanging around Hell's Kitchen all night in my Hebrew Huck Finn drag.'

THIRTY-THREE

*

The closest I could come to a pole in the loft was an old hockey stick that Ranger goalie John Davidson had given me back in some early ice age. I took that along with my cowboy hat, five cigars, and a small flashlight, and by eleven-thirty I was pouring a stiff shot of Jameson for the road into the old bullhorn.

'Don't worry about me,' I said to the cat. 'I'm totally prepared if anybody tries to come at me with a hockey puck.'

I killed the shot.

I left the cat in charge.

It was a cold, clear night and in the hack on my way to Hell's Kitchen, my mind seemed to be becoming rather colder and clearer as well. Was Ratso's supposed confession, his unusual behavior, and his strange request to speak to, of all the legions of lawyers in this world, Moie Hamburger, merely the result of remorse at the death of his friend Bramson? Or was there yet more that trusty old Dr Watson had not revealed to his lonely friend Sherlock?

It was true that Kent Perkins was a big boy, in more ways than one, but what was I getting him into here? If he weren't as smart as he was he could've passed for a near-perfect good ol' boy and the wingspan of good ol' boys isn't too long in the city. Was it fair for me to place him in a situation in which his life was clearly at risk and he was totally out of his depth? Was it fair for me to put myself in such a position? What would Ruth Buzzi or the cat say if they'd heard about the Chinatown incident?

By the time my hockey stick and I had gotten out of the cab I'd decided that after tonight Kent and I should not continue this deadly cat-and-mouse game with the dark operatives of Bimini Corporation. What was required was a more comprehensive understanding of what was going on behind the scenes. Tedious as it was, I needed to talk further with Ratso, which might prove difficult, since his lawyer had apparently now slapped an embargo on all visitors. I also needed to communicate and coordinate things, if possible, with Cooperman, and lastly, bring the whole thing out into the open through a McGovern column in the *Daily News*. These were definitely my next moves, I thought, as I walked to the little coffee shop on the corner, but first I owed it to Kent to see what, if anything, he'd been able to turn up tonight.

There were several shadowy figures loitering around and there was something that looked very much like duck vomit on the floor near the doorway, but otherwise, it appeared to be Hell's Kitchen's version of a clean, well-lighted place. There was no maître d', of course, but if the customer you were looking for was Kent Perkins, there was never any problem picking him out in a crowd. On this occasion it was even easier, since almost nobody else was in the place.

'Well,' I said, once I'd ordered some coffee and stowed the hockey stick under the table, 'I'm glad to see neither of us has joined a fundamentalist religious cult yet.'

'We came about as close as you can get this afternoon in Chinatown.'

'No shit.'

'Let me tell you what I have planned for this evening's entertainment. I think you'll find it enormously exciting.'

'As my friend John McCall always says: "Maybe you could just bring me some back on a piece of dry toast." '

Perkins laughed rather loudly. I've always believed that people who laugh loudly in restaurants are usually not very happy. Of course, that may only apply to crowded, upscale restaurants. On the other hand, Perkins could've merely been nervous. There was also the very slight possibility that he found my remarks humorous.

'Speaking of dry toast,' he said, 'don't order a hamburger here.'

I got out a cigar and began going through my preignition protocol in an effort to settle my nerves. I was still a little shaken, I suppose, about the spinning-pig experience that afternoon. I had a lingering idea in my head that if we weren't very careful, the next two spinning pigs were going to be me and Kent Perkins.

'Look,' I said, with some intensity, 'I want to know *how* and *why* we're breaking into this underground garage tonight.' If I was destined to be a spinning pig, I was at least entitled to know the reasons behind it.

'First of all,' said Perkins, as if he were talking to a small child, 'we're not breaking into the underground garage. We're breaking a light beam that will permit us to enter the garage. And here's why we're doing it.'

He slipped an envelope across the table to me and I slipped my butt-cutter out of my pocket, and, while I circumcised my cigar, observed that the envelope was addressed to the Bimini Corporation. I extracted a piece of paper from inside the envelope concomitantly with taking the phlegm-colored Bic lighter

111

that had been in the family about forty-eight hours out of my no-hunting vest. I lit the cigar and looked at the note.

'This document came into my possession,' said Kent, 'with the help of the fork on my Swiss Army knife. There was a good bit of mail building up under the door of Bimini's suite, but this was the only piece close enough for me to reach and pull out without having to remain in the hallway so long that I'd have to start paying rent.'

The note, which, judging from the date, was already a week old, was simply a notice to Bimini to move the black Lincoln-Continental from parking space A12 or else it would be towed.

'The car's still there,' said Perkins. 'You can just see it if you stand close against the building and look in the driveway mirror.'

'Obviously, no one's been in the offices for a while.'

'Well, they may come in once a week. They may never come back. All we know is that the car was still there half an hour ago. And if there's two things I'm good at it's people and cars.'

'If there's two things I'm good at it's cats and cigars. But I'm sure we can find some common ground.'

'We already have some common ground,' said Perkins rather severely. 'Somebody tried to whack us in broad daylight this afternoon in Chinatown. We don't know who's behind the Bimini Corporation, but whoever it is sure knows us. And that kind of ruthless desperation tactic tells me we're on the right trail. It also means that somebody sure as hell doesn't want your friend Ratso to find his mother.'

'Well, I'll be damned,' I said, puffing the cigar thoughtfully. 'Maybe Ratso really *is* an heir to the Goodman Egg Noodle fortune.'

THIRTY-FOUR

*

It's not difficult for an underground parking garage to look fairly evil at midnight, and this one didn't have to try too hard. It was a down-curving driveway with an iron gate that led beneath the cynical sidewalks of Manhattan and, for all anybody knew, could've been the first circle of hell. So could a lot of other things in Manhattan. At Kent's instructions, I leaned close against the building and, sure enough, there was the black Lincoln, luxuriating in its own stubbornness like a particularly pious protester in front of an abortion clinic.

The streets and sidewalks were anything but empty at this hour, and I asked Perkins if he didn't think we ought to wait awhile, like until the year 2013. 'I'm not worried about being seen,' he said. 'I've already called the police.'

'You did what?' I said, almost dropping my hockey stick.

'I told them I was with Westside Security. They're the ones who handle this carpark. I said we'd be working on the system on and off tonight. That's just a precaution in case we set off the alarm instead of opening the gate.'

'You think the police believed it?'

'Why not? I told you I was good with people. I got the three-hundred-pound black lady down at the mail drop to give me the form for Bimini Corporation so I could add additional mailing instructions. Of course, I had to work at it a little. Told her how much I appreciated the long, hard hours she was working. Even went out and brought her a sweet-potato pie. Then she gave me the form and on it was the address of this place. Now all we've got to do is open this damn gate.'

'Too bad there isn't a night watchman. You could bring him a strawberry parfait.'

'One thing you've got to love about New York,' said Kent, as he hunkered down his large form in the middle of the driveway in front of the gate. 'Nobody sees or gives a damn about anything.'

'You'd better hope that applies also to whoever's behind the Bimini Corporation.'

'All signs point to them wanting to stay the hell away from here. I'm beginning to suspect I know why.'

'Would you care to share your suspicions with your little Jewish brother?'

If Perkins heard me, he gave no indication. He moved from side to side, still in the squatting position, holding the bars at about kneecap level and peering intently into the darkness, his gaze shifting from one side of the underground chamber to the other. I lit a fresh cigar and waited, puffing quietly by the side of the building, and blowing the smoke now and then in the direction of happy young couples or that very rare specimen, the joggerus midnightus idioticus. It was getting late in the year for them but I did manage to see a few.

'What do you plan to do?' I said at last. 'Squat there all night like an ape at the zoo?'

Perkins did not look up. If anything, he stared more intently through the iron bars. He held his arm out, palm up, in my general direction.

'Hockey stick,' he said.

I handed him the hockey stick.

'Cowboy hat,' he said.

I handed him the cowboy hat, which he placed on top of the large end of the hockey stick so that it could be moved along the ground, which gave the thing a rather uncanny resemblance to one of Cecil Hausenfluck's little children.

'Dr Perkins,' I said, 'are you sure that amputating the patient at the neck was the appropriate surgical procedure?'

Perkins did not respond but continued marching the ridiculous little mechanism closer to the infra-red beam. Finally, extending his arms fully inside the bars of the gate, he found himself just out of reach of the light beam.

'Six more inches and you would've been king,' I said.

'Horseshit and wild honey!' said Kent Perkins rather vehemently. 'One of us is going to have to Frisbee the cowboy hat.'

'That'd be your department,' I said. 'You're from California.'

'You understand what's at risk, don't you? If I toss the hat and miss the light beam, we not only don't get the gate open but, also, you'll probably never see that hat again.'

'I'd hate to see it flattened by a Mustang. Or stomped by a Cherokee.'

'Or rear-ended by a Probe,' said Kent. 'Maybe some executive will wear it to mow his lawn in Connecticut.'

'People don't mow lawns in Connecticut,' I said. 'They go to golf courses.'

'So he'll wear it to the golf course, then get tired of it and sell it for a few bucks at a garage sale.'

'People don't have garage sales in Connecticut,' I said. 'He'd probably give it to the Salvation Army or the Hadassah Thrift Shop, depending, of course, on the particular nature of his deep religious affiliations.'

'Then some Puerto Rican pimp picks it up cheap,' said Perkins, 'and gives it to a red-headed whore with a gold tooth in Spanish Harlem.'

'Who wears a peach-colored dress.'

'And who throws it in along with a Japanese basket-fuck to an executive from Connecticut, who loses it in this underground garage and it gets flattened by a Mustang.'

'It's a reasonable scenario,' I said.

'Let's hit it the first time,' said Perkins.

And he Frisbeed the cowboy hat.

For a second or two there was silence as the hat sailed across time and geography as fatefully as Columbus sailing a wishing well. Then we heard an almost medieval clanking sound. Either the gate was opening or Columbus was dying in chains. Neither event would've raised an eyebrow in New York.

'We'll be inside that Lincoln quicker than a minnow can swim a dipper,' said Perkins.

The next thing I knew, he was fooling around with the lock on the passenger-side door of the Lincoln, and I was hustling my ass down the drive to look for my cowboy hat. By the time I'd found it, checked it out for grease stains, put it on my head, and walked over to Kent, he had the door open.

'What took you so long?' I said.

'Sorry, Kink. It's been a while since I've committed a felony and I wanted to be sure I didn't scratch the finish.'

Perkins made a quick check inside the car; then his big, blond head disappeared under the darkness of the dashboard. I made a quick check around the garage and found no one stirring; then my kinky little head disappeared in a blue cloud of protective cigar smoke. All my life I'd wanted to have a big head like Perkins or McGovern. I had a chronic case of head envy and there was nothing I could do about it but walk around the garage with my hockey stick and look out for cops or robbers or the boys from the Bimini Corporation, who didn't give a damn what size head I had as long as they could take it off my shoulders and move it to the suburbs.

While Perkins was messing around under the dash-board either hot-wiring the car or looking for used gum, I jotted down the license number of the Lincoln and any other sticker or decal numbers I could find. It's always good to make yourself useful. I was just putting my little notebook away when the engine started.

'Hop in,' said Kent. 'Let's go egg Mary Goodman's house.'

'If we knew where it was,' I said.

Kent opened the glove compartment, removed some papers inside, glanced briefly at them, and put them inside his coat pocket.

'Might make for some good light summer reading,' he said.

'I'll wait for the movie.'

Then Kent reached back into the glove compartment and pushed a button and the trunk of the car began to open slowly upward, like the lid of a crypt. Since I hadn't smelled anything in over fifteen years, Kent was the first to realize that something was rotten in the state of Denmark.

'I don't know what's in there,' he said, 'but it'd stink a buzzard off a gut wagon.'

We both walked with somewhat measured tread to the back of the car and peered into the trunk. The bloated face of death was smiling up at us like a friendly AmWay representative. We weren't going to need to refer to a Martindale-Hubble directory anymore.

We'd found Moie Hamburger.

THIRTY-FIVE
*

Cooperman was not happy to see the hockey stick or the stiff in the trunk. He'd seen a lot of stiffs in a lot of trunks in his time, and he didn't appear to appreciate my thoughtfulness in getting in touch with him about seeing one more. I'd been under the mistaken impression that this one, just possibly, might lend some slight confirmation to my contention that somebody was indeed out there who wished very much for Ratso not to find his birth mother. I also took the opportunity to bend Cooperman's somewhat jaundiced ear with my account of the Chinatown attack upon Kent and myself, as well as to reiterate my close encounter with the krautmobile in Miami.

Not only had Cooperman and Fox taken the call, which was

out of their precinct, rather grudgingly, they did not seem to feel that the rather ignominious adjournment of this lawyer's life made it any less plausible that Ratso had killed Jack Bramson. While Kent's engaging, Rockford-like appeal did appear to chip a little ice off Cooperman, it was mildly reassuring to see that some things never change in this funny old world. The cop-like glint in his eyes told me that my own rapport with the vaunted detective-sergeant was about the same as if he'd suddenly encountered Spinoza stumbling through the Bowery.

'*Two* fucking cowboys,' he said, after briefly surveying the garage and the Lincoln.

'And *one* hockey stick,' said Fox brightly.

'This was the lawyer,' I said, gesturing toward the open trunk, 'whose father made all the arrangements for Ratso's adoption. He's also the one Ratso tried to call from the precinct house when he was first arrested. Unless, of course, in his state of extreme remorse and depression, he was merely mumbling the name of the dead man's father, the person he may have blamed for originally setting all his problems into motion.'

'This certainly explains why the lawyer never called him back,' said Cooperman, chuckling dryly to himself as he stared down at the grotesque vision before us.

'You'd have thought,' said Fox, as he stepped out of the shadows, 'that he'd at least have had the courtesy to make a trunk call.'

Kent Perkins looked on wide-eyed, making an awkward effort at a smile. I didn't even try. Other than Fox asking a few questions about my hockey stick, he and Cooperman didn't really seem to have their hearts in it either. When the local precinct dicks showed up, Cooperman and Fox left and the new guys didn't know about Ratso and didn't want to. After a cursory interview or two, Kent and I were allowed to bug out for the dugout and we didn't waste any time getting out of those catacombs.

'Shit,' said Kent, once we'd gotten into the cab. 'I forgot to give the cops those papers from the glove compartment.'

'That's the best news I've heard all day,' I said. 'Let's go over to Sarge's Deli and do a little cramming for the final exam.'

It was after three by the time we got to Sarge's, but a second wind seemed to be blowing in from someplace and you could see the pages of the newspapers riffling on the sidewalk as if they were being turned by invisible hands. Third Avenue was pretty empty of traffic and so was Sarge's, but it was still three forty-five before my pastrami sandwich came in for a belly landing on table number 47.

'My father's theory about restaurants applies here,' I said, checking the hockey stick under the table.

'What'd he say? Stay out of Sarge's?'

'No, Sarge's is okay. The food is good and it gives you time to think. Plus, it's a good place to see and be seen at this hour of the night.' I looked up at the diminished parade of customers drifting close by our table like termagant ghosts. Kent nodded briefly and continued eating his bagel.

'What's your father's theory?' he said.

'Well, Tom's restaurant theory was first propounded in Austin, Texas, but certainly has universal applications. It's really very simple. His theory is: "The fewer the customers, the slower the service." '

'I'd hate to be the only people in the place,' said Kent, as he removed the papers from the glove compartment of the Lincoln and laid them down next to a large complimentary bowl of pickles.

'Do you think there's anything here?' I said, gesturing at the documents with my lips like a native of Borneo. 'Any paper trail we can follow?'

'It's going to be difficult,' he said. 'The ignition lock was punched out.'

'So?'

'So it means the car was almost certainly stolen.'

'Terrific,' I said. 'So these papers and maps, Triple A crap, and gas receipts all belong to some little old lady who only went out to bingo games.'

'I'm afraid so,' said Kent, 'but this towing company receipt for fixing a flat tire appears to be more recent than the dates on the gas receipts. This might be what we're looking for. Remember Perkins's Theory of Stolen Vehicles, which I propounded in Los Angeles about the time Professor Friedman was propounding his Theory of Restaurant Service.'

'Which is?' I said, with an almost Gandhi-like effort at patience.

'When you steal a car you don't check for a spare.'

'To that theory,' I said, 'I'd like to add a possible corollary.'

'Which is?' said Perkins.

'You also don't check for a spare,' I said, 'if you know that it's covered by a rapidly decomposing Hamburger.'

THIRTY-SIX

*

Beaver & Son Towing Service was a twenty-four-hour operation. So were we. It was about a ten-minute cab ride, and when we got there it looked like the towing company had towed everything away but a lot of fence and a small temporary office set up in a trailer wedged between two larger buildings. There was a light burning in the trailer.

'Do you think Ruth's going to be angry that you've stayed out all night?' I said, as we got out of the cab.

'Yes,' said Kent.

'You *did* call her?'

'Of course. She's very understanding, but she also gets very angry. She's the world's only angry, understanding wife.'

'That's why I have a cat.'

As we walked up the little alleyway that led to the trailer, blocked out on both sides by big buildings under a Manhattan sky that had never held a harvest moon, with the towing receipt in the inside pocket of my coat, I thought, not for the first time, how much of life hangs by a silver thread of spit, by a fragile black chain of frog eggs across a country pond. This had to be the end of the road, I figured.

If this lead didn't pan, I could send all the documents to the cops and maybe they'd find the old lady in time to get the car back to her before the next bingo game. The cops weren't interested in the Bimini Corporation, and there was no way we were going to crack it without their help. There was no one else to go to. Eliot Ness was worm bait and George Smiley was probably sitting on some lichen-stained park bench feeding sparrows somewhere across the old herring pond. Whatever chance there'd been to pry anything out of Moie Hamburger had disappeared when Kent Perkins pushed the little button inside the glove compartment of the Lincoln. A Lincoln was a good car to die in, I thought. I remembered with a fleeting smile something the great French author and philosopher Jean Genet reportedly had once said as he was being driven around Chicago on a long-ago speaking tour. 'Only in America,' he'd commented, 'would they name an automobile "Galaxy".'

The cold and rather grimy tendrils of dawn were foisting themselves upon my bloodshot eyeballs like a cedar branch rattling against an ancient, rusty windowscreen. Maybe it's only some sense of cosmic hindsight, but I seemed to remember thinking, as we closed in on the place, that the little trailer, indeed, held something important for us. We peered in a window and saw a large, burly guy facing away from us, squatting over what appeared to be a small radiator.

'Never squat with your spurs on,' I said to Perkins.

'If he showed any more butt cleavage,' said Kent, 'he'd have to join a union.'

As we climbed the steps of a tiny porch, we could see through the trailer the tow truck parked in a scraggly backyard, gleaming like a crown jewel in the recycled light of the city. Even standing still there was something about the vehicle that gave you the notion of an oncoming train. On the side of the truck, in bright script, read the emblem: *Beaver and Son Towing Service.* We knocked on the door of the trailer, and the guy jumped up like a bottle rocket. He gave us a careful fish eye out the window and either he liked Kent's big, friendly Texas smile or my cowboy hat or else he was a hockey fan, because he opened the door.

'You guys liked to scare the shit out of me,' he said.

'Don't tell me,' said Kent Perkins, 'that at five o'clock in the morning in this godforsaken city I recognize a Texas accent?'

'Travis Beaver,' said the guy, sticking out a big hand in Kent's direction. 'Weatherford, Texas.'

'Hell,' said Kent, genuinely pleased, 'my name's Kent Perkins. I'm from Azle, Texas. Kink, Azle and Weatherford are both just spittin' distance from Fort Worth. Me and Travis might've played on opposing football teams. I played left tackle for the Azle Hornets.'

'I was right guard for the Weatherford Kangaroos,' said Beaver with growing excitement.

'Sting the Kangaroos!' shouted Kent.

'Swat the Hornets!' shouted Beaver.

Then he suddenly put a finger to his lips and gestured toward the back of the trailer where a small bundle appeared to be lying on an army cot. Kent and I tiptoed over and saw a tousle-headed, freckle-faced boy about ten years old, sound asleep.

'Beaver and Son,' whispered Beaver proudly, as he came over to join us. 'That's Travis Beaver, Jr.'

For just a moment the three of us watched the kid sleep. He

looked like one of Peter Pan's Lost Boys, I thought. When you think of Peter Pan you're really thinking of Mary Martin. I thought of Mary Martin. And I remembered something in a dollop of cosmic trailer insight. Mary Martin had come from Weatherford, Texas. I leaned on my hockey stick for spiritual support. Maybe, dear God, Mary Martin had once been a cheerleader for the Weatherford Kangaroos. Maybe she'd once stood in a line with the other blond, young, small-town girls and the head cheerleader had said: 'Ready?' and the girls had all answered together: 'Ohh-*kay!*'

For no reason except possibly the hour, an old country music song popped into my head:

> *Just a small-town girl 'til she learned to twirl*
> *Then she set the world on fire*
> *Like a drive-in Cinderella*
> *in a Chevy named desire*
> *So leave your teddy bear at the county fair*
> *Honey, Hollywood's on the phone*
> *For a small-town girl from a small-town world*
> *you're a long, long way from home.*

I must've taken a brief vertical power nap, because suddenly I noticed that Perkins and Beaver were drinking coffee and talking earnestly at a table and I was still gawking at the kid with John Davidson's wooden memento high-sticking me in the sternum.

A short time later I was standing by the table with a cup of steaming coffee in front of me and Kent Perkins smiling to beat the band.

'Tell him, Travis,' said Kent.

'I remember the guy you're looking for,' said Beaver. 'Car was a black, late-model Lincoln with a flat tire and he said he didn't have a spare. Had to tow him and he also paid me for a new tire. This was about a week ago.'

'What'd he look like?' I said, drinking my coffee and holding my breath and, in so doing, coming dangerously close to a Danny Thomas coffee spit.

'Big fellow with long black hair and a dark, bushy beard. Gave me two C-notes and I told him that I wanted to see his driver's license because I've been getting so many counterfeit C-notes. He said no and I said then I'll just take the goddamn tire back off the car and he finally said okay and showed me his driver's license.'

Now I was definitely balancing on the edge of my hockey stick. Beaver was going for the hat trick and I wasn't about to try to check him.

'It's kind of foggy in my mind,' Beaver continued, 'but I know the address wasn't in the city. A New York driver's license but not from the city. Kind of an Indian-sounding place. Sounded a little bit like Chappaquiddick.'

'Maybe Ted Kennedy finally got around to calling a tow truck,' said Kent.

Beaver laughed. I realized once again how good Kent was at the game of painlessly pulling things out of people. Beaver was at a crucial point of breaking the case wide open and Kent had him relaxed and talking to us like old friends.

'What was the name on the driver's license?' said Kent.

Travis Beaver set down his coffee cup, put his hand on his head, and closed his eyes to concentrate. He held that position long enough to germinate several generations of fruit flies. I looked at Kent. Kent looked at me. We both looked at Travis Beaver. Then, still keeping his hand on his head, Beaver opened his eyes.

'Donald Goodman,' he said. 'Does that sound right?'

THIRTY-SEVEN

There are about a million places in New York State that have
Indian names. The reason for this is that there once were about
a zillion Indians living thereabouts until they traded the island
of Manhattan for twenty-six dollars and a string of beads,
which, as anyone who's visited New York recently can attest,
was probably the best deal the Indians ever made. Every time I
think of Indian names I'm reminded of the legend of the young
warrior who came to the chief to inquire if he could change his
name. If you've ever studied Indian lore you're no doubt familiar with the chief's sage reply: 'Why do you ask, Two Dogs
Fucking?'

Of course, when you narrow it down to Indian names that
sound kind of like Chappaquiddick, there's not all that much to
work with. There's Chappaquitdick, the summer resort from
which Richard Nixon resigned the presidency. There's Chappa-
quidproquo, the well-known watering hole for corporate
attorneys. There's the popular spot where all the tourists
invariably flock, Chappanudnick. And, finally, there's the little
Indian village in which the natives were reported to have inter-
married with an early group of irritated Italian immigrants,
Chappamyass.

As I sat with my feet up on the desk the following afternoon,
there was only one Indian name written down on my Big Chief
tablet. This I now circled. Then I smiled like a self-satisfied
serial killer and lifted Sherlock's porcelain cap to take a fresh
cigar out of his porcelain head.

I put the Big Chief tablet on the desk and got up and walked
over to the refrigerator, stopping long enough to extract a bag
from the latest shipment of coffee beans that Kathy De Palma
had sent me from Maui. With the unlit cigar in my mouth for

general ballast, I went rapidly through a series of household activities, many thoughts percolating in my mind, not the least of which was the name on the Big Chief tablet and what it represented. I believed it to be, at least geographically speaking, the solution of the case.

I ground the coffee beans and fed them into the espresso machine with the facile grace of a Roman soldier throwing Christians to the lions. As I waited for the machine to move into overdrive, I smiled up at the little black puppet head on top of the refrigerator.

'Alas, poor Yorick,' I said, 'you've seen very little action of late. The visitors to our humble quarters have been few. But I suspect, my dear friend, that all of that is about to change.'

The little black puppet head smiled back down at me. It was not the big, broad, Texas smile Kent Perkins often utilized to mesmerize the populace. But it was not without its own simple charm. Unwavering. No guile. No hidden agenda. If I stayed there forever gazing upon that little ebony face it would mean a life lived looking only at the Greek mask of comedy, sheltered and safe from sorrow, never knowing the tragic countenance of this world. But somebody had to feed the cat.

I fed the cat.

Soon the smell of Hawaiian coffee filled the loft and I paced back and forth with the unlit cigar while the cat ate the tuna and the pigeons shit on the windowsills and the puppet head continued to smile warmly at the far wall upon which a picture of a ballet dancer had been hung by some former tenant, no doubt, who, for all I knew, may have hung himself as well. That would go a long way toward explaining some of the spiritual ambience I'd been noticing in the loft.

But it'd been a good, purposeful day, all in all. I'd green-lighted McGovern on the human interest piece on Ratso's personal quest for his long-lost birth mother. After no small amount of cajoling I'd convinced McGovern to eighty-six the bit about Ratso's current place of residence.

'We want a big, splashy spread on this,' I'd told him earlier that afternoon, 'and we need it to run within the next forty-eight hours.'

'That's up to the editor,' McGovern had said.

'Fuck the editor,' I'd told him.

'My sentiments precisely,' he'd said.

As well as getting McGovern cranked up and into operation, Simmons had also reported from the field. He'd been to see Ratso a number of times and, apparently, had gotten him in touch with a high-powered lawyer who Simmons felt might possibly get him out on bail.

'Ratso's showing marked improvement,' Simmons had said.

'If he vomited on your head it'd be marked improvement,' I'd commented at the time.

Finally, I'd spoken to Stephanie, who'd expressed growing interest in becoming a part of the mother hunt, especially now that, in her words, 'it seems to be going somewhere'. I'd also talked with Kent and we'd agreed that we'd have to swing into action soon.

'There's a strange thing about dusty old investigations like this one,' Kent had said. 'Remember, they're all open cases. That means there's usually someone in the shadows who doesn't want them ever to be solved.'

'This time,' I'd said, 'we know who that someone is. And I'm pretty damn sure I know *where* that someone is.'

When the coffee was ready, I drew a steaming cupful into my old Imus in the Morning mug and took Imus's mug, the coffee, and myself over to the desk. I took a sip of the coffee and for a moment through the steam I saw Robert Louis Stevenson sitting under a banyan tree with Princess Kaiulani. Princess Kaiulani, the last princess of Hawaii, did not have much time to gaze at a smiling puppet head. Her prince never came, she died tragically young, living only long enough to see her kingdom tumble down all around her. That is why good Hawaiian coffee always tastes a little bitter, as well as a little better than any other in the world.

I took another sip or two and studied again the one Indian word on the Big Chief tablet. The word was 'Chappaqua', an Indian name for a place in New York that would sound like Chappaquiddick to someone from out of state. As it happened, I knew the place well. Many moons ago, I'd lived there myself.

I struck a kitchen match on the leg of my old blue jeans and set fire to the cigar. I kept the tip of the cigar ever so slightly above the level of the flame and, as I did so, I could almost feel the noose tightening ever so slightly around Donald Goodman's neck.

THIRTY-EIGHT
*

Two mornings later McGovern's story hit the streets, and shortly after that Kent Perkins and I hit the road for Chappaqua. We stopped only long enough in the Village to pick up Mick Brennan, photographer extraordinaire, at a little dive near where the Bells of Hell used to be. The Bells of Hell had been known for many things and one of them was the night McGovern's eyeball popped out of his head when some guy blindsided him as he was sitting at the bar. McGovern contends that the eyeball popped right out of his skullhouse and hung there attached only to a viscous mucuslike connective tissue. He walked the eyeball, holding it in the palm of his hand, to the emergency room of St Vincent's Hospital, where (of great spiritual import to McGovern) Bessie Smith had died. He waited two hours in the emergency room while doctors worked furiously on other matters like separating people who'd gotten stuck together hosing. Eventually, a nurse spotted McGovern and the eyeball was popped back into his large head, larger even than Kent Perkins's, and he was able to return to the Bells of Hell just in time for final call.

The story, of course, had almost no relevance to the journey we were embarking upon except possibly as a mute reminder to keep our eyes out for trouble. There'd never been much trouble in Chappaqua and most people there probably wouldn't have recognized it if it'd ridden in on a large black hippopotamus, but, as we would soon find out, all that was getting ready to change.

Having picked up Brennan, who was sporting a camera and lens that would've given the spoiler a run for its money, Kent aimed the rent-a-car down the Saw Mill River Parkway and we headed out for a quiet day in suburbia. Brennan and Perkins were about as different as two people could be, having virtually nothing in common, so I reasoned that they would get along well together and they did. This was important because they were both to be key players in a drama that could very well place all our lives at stake. For finding Mary Goodman, I was now certain, meant dealing with Donald Goodman, a man I believed had already dealt with Jack Bramson and Moie Hamburger and would've already dealt with Kent and myself had destiny not shuffled the cards at the last minute. And if there's one thing I know about destiny it is that you can't count on it forever.

Over the past few days, Kent and I had hammered out a plan that we hoped would enable us to find Mary Goodman and gather evidence against Donald, who we believed was either her son or nephew and who obviously had a great deal to lose if Ratso got together with Mary. Finding the Goodman estate had actually been the easy part. I'd called my friend Sal Lorello, who, as well as having been my road manager for many years, had also run a limo service out of Chappaqua. Sal had driven everybody who was anybody in Westchester after being on the road with me had fairly well driven him over the edge. Then Cleve had taken over as road manager and, of course, wound up in residence at the Pilgrim State Mental Hospital. Ratso, who'd accompanied me on practically all of my forays into crime solving, was now a registered guest of the NYPD. Good help, I reflected, as we pulled into sleepy Chappaqua, was hard to get these days. As Willie Nelson once told me: 'You've got to be able to move on to the next big town without slashing your wrists.'

'Hard to believe I lived here for two years,' I said, as we drove past the quaint little shops and houses.

'Hard to believe you stayed the weekend, mate,' said Brennan.

It hadn't taken Sal Lorello long to call me back with rough, hopefully accurate, directions to Mary Goodman's estate. Sal had never met Mary and didn't know anyone who had. Word around town was that she was an extremely wealthy, Howard Hughes-like, semi-invalid, who spent a lot of time in her garden but otherwise almost never left the sanctuary of the estate, which was, in fact, a modern-day castle.

We drove through Chappaqua and headed east on a smaller road, then turned to the right on a still smaller one. Kent stopped the car on a little bluff and studied the landscape with a pair of binoculars.

'Did you bring along your bird book?' I said to Brennan.

'Jesus Christ,' said Kent suddenly. 'The place looks like an Irish castle.'

'That it does, mate,' said Brennan, following along through the camera lens. 'Goodman, you know, is a well-respected Irish family name.' Brennan winked in my direction.

'Just don't drive this rent-a-car into the moat,' I said, as Perkins shooed Brennan and me into the car like baby chicks and roared off in the direction of the castle.

We found a small copse of trees to the side of the road that enabled us to see the main entrance and the front lawns of the place without being too conspicuous. The vision was one of Xanadu-like opulence.

'Mick,' I said, 'your job is to work your way around the perimeter and take unobtrusive *National Enquirer*-type shots. I know you've never been unobtrusive in your life, but give it a try. The photos may be very helpful when we come back in a few days to implement phase two of the plan, the penetration of the castle.'

'Which is going to be a bitch,' said Kent. 'There's a heavily manned guardhouse and enough goons walking around to protect the Pope. Lot of security for a little old lady in a garden, no matter who she is. Of course, in this kind of operation, you'd never go in the main entrance.'

'What's this you've marked in yellow here, mate?' asked Brennan, as he looked over Kent's map of the general vicinity.

'That's the local hospital,' said Kent with a smile. 'This kind of operation, it's always a good idea to know just where it is.'

'Bloody terrific, mate,' said Brennan. But he was already adjusting his lenses.

'You know, the one thing I don't understand about this,' Brennan was saying, 'is why – '

'Hold the weddin',' I said.

At that moment, out the front drive past the guard-house came a long blue Rolls Royce driven by a big, burly man with long, disheveled black hair and a bushy black beard. The man and the vehicle rolled inexorably through the chill afternoon with the fluid ruthless motion of a maestro walking onto the podium. One glance and you knew that not even a brick wall would stop him. He was the same large, hairy mammal who'd almost left me for road-kill as he'd stormed out of Moie Hamburger's office.

'Get him, Mick,' I said.

Mick snapped away almost as fast as a fashion photographer. But getting Donald Goodman on film and getting him off-camera were two distinctly different matters. There's no such thing as innocent wealth, I thought. And on Goodman, wealth looked positively evil. A sudden sinking feeling came over me as I realized the Herculean nature of our task.

'The cops just aren't interested in Donald Goodman,' I said. 'With all his money and power I'm not sure by ourselves that we'll ever be able to catch him.'

'As my old dad in Texas used to tell me,' said Kent, ' "Justice rides a slow horse, but it always overtakes." '

'That's well and good,' said Brennan. 'But the old nag's never going to overtake that fuckwit in the Rolls.'

The blue Rolls Royce sped up the little road with the sinister grace and finality of a brush stroke on the canvas of the devil. We crouched behind the rent-a-car and watched Donald Goodman until he was out of sight. In that moment I thought again of Cecil Hausenfluck's words describing the man who huffed and puffed and blew Ratso's door down. In my mind I knew with a certainty that this was the same man.

'That's got to be him,' I said. 'He's the Big Bad Wolf.'

'If he is, mate,' said Brennan, setting down his camera, 'let's bloody well hope we're not the Three Little Pigs.'

THIRTY-NINE
*

We left Mick Brennan and his camera hiding behind a large elm tree with instructions to circle slowly around the side of the place and shoot anything that moved.

'Don't get caught,' said Kent. 'If you do, I'm afraid you'll be on your own.'

'Have done most of my life, mate,' said Brennan, and he set out through the woods.

'We'll pick you up in a few hours,' I said, but I wasn't sure he heard me.

Kent and I drove the car around to the rear of the big place, where Kent stopped and donned a dark blue tie and a cap that read: SECURITY. With his overcoat and clipboard he appeared to be someone to be reckoned with.

'How do I look?' he said, as he got out of the car.

'I'd hire you.'

'You already did.'

We waited and watched for a while in the bushes that abutted a narrow driveway. Traffic here seemed much busier than it had at the main entrance.

'The good news,' said Kent, 'is that a setup of this size requires lots of coming and going by way of the servants' entrance and almost certainly a heavy turnover of personnel. That's going to make it easier for us when we make our move.'

Kent paused for a moment as some kind of electrician's van pulled into the drive. As it did, an old landscaper's pickup and a butcher's van were pulling out.

'Jesus,' I said, 'everybody's here but Beaver and Son.'

'I'll just join the party,' said Kent, picking up his clipboard and striding confidently up the driveway. 'I'll be back in an hour or so.'

'What am I supposed to do?' I shouted after him.

'Just loiter around. See what you can see.'

'Have done, mate,' I said. 'Most of my life.'

I walked back to the car, got in, and took out a fresh cigar and fired her up. My problem with loitering around this place was that Kent Perkins looked like the chief of security and I looked like Lazarus after the fifth day. Well, I was on my own and I'd just have to deal with it. I wasn't quite sure what Perkins's idea was, but he'd told me it was a good one and I believed him. Then I looked up at the seemingly impregnable walls and turrets of the Goodman estate and began to have my doubts. Then I puffed on my cigar, watched the traffic come and go through the servants' entrance, and forgot all about it. When it came to loitering and daydreaming, I was definitely aces.

I was gazing lazily up through some palm trees somewhere in the South Seas when somebody rapped on my window with the barrel of a gun and I just about swallowed my cigar. A moment later, I saw, to my great relief, Kent Perkins's big, smiling face filling up my window.

'Excuse me, sir,' he said. 'Could you tell me how to get to the Statue of Liberty?'

'Sure,' I said. 'The first thing you do is get the hell out of here.'

As we began the rather tedious process of ferreting Mick Brennan out of the woodwork without appearing too suspicious to Goodman's goons, Kent filled me in on his little infiltration maneuver.

'Donald Goodman's gone away for a week on business. That gives us a good window to work with.'

'That's great,' I said. 'The last one we had got blown out in Chinatown.'

'What I did was turn certain delivery and service people away until further notice. Mr Goodman's orders.'

'I hope you took rather copious notes of who they were.'

'Got all that. But we're going to need some help if you want to come back later in the week and replace them with our own people.'

'That's no problem,' I said. 'McGovern and Brennan, if we ever find him, will be happy to help out. And Stephanie DuPont's been harassing me to get involved in this case. Wait till you see her. Maybe she could pass as an outcall massage girl.'

'Good idea. Maybe I'll call her myself.'

'What would Ruthie do if she found out?'

'Probably just detach the Spoiler with a machete and donate it to Engine Company Number Nine.'

After searching high and low for Brennan, we found him low, shivering under the same elm tree where we'd left him.

'Shot five rolls,' he said, once he'd gotten into the car. 'Lots of men with guns and maids with tea trays.'

'Any sign of an old lady?' said Kent.

'None. But it wouldn't surprise me if she was holed up in there somewhere. The servants carrying tea out to the garden almost made me homesick. Anyway, you've got a small army of servants on the inside ministering to a little old lady and on the outside you've got a small army of blokes with guns trying to protect her.'

'Or what is more likely,' I said, 'trying to keep her there.'

'She must be one hell of a little old lady.'

'If she's Ratso's mother,' I said, 'anything's possible.'

Anything was indeed possible, I thought, as Perkins aimed the car back in the direction of Chappaqua. And it's just when you think you've thought of everything that anything can happen. When it does, there's always some nerd who goes around shaking his head disapprovingly and very sagely muttering: 'Anything's possible'. I vowed to myself that on this particular occasion that nerd would not be me.

'Do you think Mary Goodman's really somewhere on that estate?' said Kent, taking off his security cap and loosening his tie.

'I'd bet my life on it,' I said.

FORTY
*

On the way from Chappaqua back to the city we got caught in the mother of all traffic jams, and Kent, over Brennan's mild protestations, took the opportunity to tell a rather poignant coming-of-age story about himself as a young man in Fort Worth, Texas.

'Every time I see a Rolls Royce,' said Kent, 'I think of the first Rolls I ever owned. It was also the last. I was about twenty-two years old, a young, hotshot land speculator, and I'd made myself some bucks and I wanted to spend 'em. So I bought a beautiful new black Rolls down in Houston, spent about six hours waxing and polishing her up, and drove her to Fort Worth to show her off to my friends and in-laws from my first wife. Ruthie's seen a lot of Rolls Royces in her time. She wouldn't have been impressed.

'But the folks in Fort Worth and especially in Azle, Texas, many of them had never actually seen one. I remember as I drove through Azle, every eye was on me and that car. I was stopped at a red light and a farmer in an old pickup pulled up next to me and said: "Nice car. My daddy used to have an ol' Packard just like that."

'I drove it to my in-laws' house and parked it in the driveway and they all came out and gawked and they were very impressed. I can still see that car. It just shone like a jewel in the Texas sun.

'Anyway, next door to my wife's folks lived my favorite uncle, Uncle Rosie. Now Uncle Rosie was blind but he knew what was going on. He could call out your name just by hearing your footsteps on the sidewalk. He passed the time "watching" John Wayne movies. I think he'd "seen" every movie John Wayne ever made, probably hundreds of times. Anyway, Uncle Rosie had been very excited about seeing the Rolls Royce. This caused a problem in my young mind because I could just imagine his hands moving up and down all over the car and ruining my new wax job.

'So, with some trepidation, I left the car in my in-laws' driveway and walked next door to where Uncle Rosie lived and, sure enough, he called my name as I came walking up the sidewalk.

He was watching *She Wore a Yellow Ribbon*, starring, of course, John Wayne. He asked me if the car was here yet and I lied and told him no, but it was coming in in a couple of days.

' "I just want to feel the fancy leather on those seats," he said. "I just want to say howdy to that pretty little lady on the grille." And I thought again about my new wax job.

'Well, I told him I'd bring it right over just as soon as it arrived and I felt bad about it because the car, of course, was sitting right next door in the driveway the whole time. But it was just one of those things that happens when you're young and hopefully you learn from it and become a better person. If I had it to do over again I'd've taken Uncle Rosie by the hand and personally introduced him to the little lady on the grille and seen to it that he saw all of that car he wanted to.

'Anyway, that's not how it happened. I promised Uncle Rosie again that I'd bring the Rolls by as soon as I got it and then I left. I went home and felt like hell and decided that night that I'd go ahead and just bring the car over to him the next day, wax job be damned.

'So I woke up the next morning and I remember I was just making coffee when my wife got a call from my in-laws. Uncle Rosie had died.'

The traffic seemed to have cleared off a bit and Kent drove on with the kind of faraway look in his eyes that I thought I'd noticed several nights before when he'd been looking at Travis Beaver's sleeping son. I puffed silently on my cigar. Nobody spoke for a while. Then Brennan piped up from the backseat.

'There's a lesson in that,' he said.

'Yes, Mick?' I said. 'And what would that be?'

'Don't fuck around with blind people, mate.'

FORTY-ONE

*

'I'm not going to be an au pair girl,' said Stephanie DuPont defiantly. It was two days later and a small coordinating session was under way in the loft. We still had, according to Perkins, a four-day window to work with.

'Especially,' Stephanie continued, 'for some sick fuck in Chappaqua.'

'Sorry,' said McGovern, 'there's not much demand for au pair girls in Brooklyn.'

'Have you thought about being an outcall masseuse?' I said.

'No, turbo-dick,' said Stephanie.

'An au pair girl is what they're expecting,' said Kent Perkins, 'and an au pair is what they're going to get. So if you insist upon using that language, at least get the accent right.'

'I'd hate to have an au pair girl with *your* accent, mate,' said Brennan.

'Or yours,' said McGovern. He and Brennan had been drinking Guinness all afternoon from a large supply I'd purchased from Myers of Keswick on Hudson Street. As an accommodating host, I'd done my best to keep up with them.

'It's unfortunate,' I said, 'that Ratso and Rambam can't be with us to help plan this operation.'

'Yeah,' said McGovern. 'It's almost pleasant.'

'Rambam,' I continued, 'is jumping with the Burmese Army Paratroopers – '

'He can jump up my ass, mate.'

'And Ratso, of course, cannot be with us for reasons that all of you know.'

'And I was so looking forward,' said Stephanie, barely concealing her disgust, 'to meeting all the rest of your friends.'

'Probably,' said Kent, ignoring the previous exchanges, 'we'll make our move three days from now while Donald Goodman is still away and we have some chance of finding the old lady. Stephanie will be the au pair. Kink, McGovern, and myself will be housepainters. And Brennan will be an interior decorator.'

'Brilliant,' said Brennan. 'I'll need a beret and a little dickie.'

'You probably already have a little dickie,' said Stephanie.

'Bloody Christ,' said Mick. 'Where'd you find this brazen bird?' He gestured in Stephanie's direction by tilting slightly one of the many empty Guinness bottles standing in front of him.

'She just fluttered in the window of opportunity one morning,' I said. 'And now she's become my favorite pet albatross.'

'Shut up, Hebe,' said Stephanie sweetly.

'God, I just thought of it,' I said. 'Without Ratso and Rambam, I'm the only Jew in this whole operation!'

'That's why it may have a chance of success, mate,' said Brennan.

'If everybody just plays their part,' I said, 'everything will be fine. Mick's photos should be developed by tonight and that ought to be a big help. McGovern's story in the newspaper has definitely got the town buzzing. It may even be part of the reason Donald Goodman hit the road. We're going to almost certainly make our move within three days' time, so get whatever outfits, vehicles, or props you think you might need. And remember, we have but one primary purpose in this adventure. Find Mary Goodman. After we ascertain that she's safe and sound, we can let the cops deal with Donald Goodman, her nephew or son or whatever he is.'

'Have you considered,' said McGovern, 'that he could be her husband?'

'There's certainly enough money involved,' said Kent. 'It's entirely possible.'

'So she may be robbing the cradle,' said Brennan, with a wicked smile. 'Like the Kinkster.'

Stephanie looked at Brennan with a gaze that would have

withered a pressed flower. 'Don't mention Kinky,' she said, 'when I'm trying to relax.'

'One thing I can't emphasize enough,' said Kent Perkins, with an earnestness and a new intensity in his voice, as he stood tall above the little group. 'This is a mission of a decidedly dangerous nature. Donald Goodman will not be there on the day we infiltrate the place, but if he's who we think he is, he's already killed two people and just missed killing two more – me and Kinky. We don't want to run up against his security goons and, if all goes well, we shouldn't have to. Except for the housepainters, McGovern, Kink, and myself, we will all be working separately, but actually, of course, we'll all be working together. And a chain is only as strong as its weakest link.'

'That's McGovern,' said Brennan.

'Hush,' said Stephanie.

Kent raised his hands to quiet the crowd. He gazed briefly at each face like a commander sending his men on a mission from which he believes they may never return.

'And remember this,' Perkins continued, staring off Patton-like into some middle distance that only he could see, 'I will be armed. If you run into trouble, I will do all I can to help you. Kink will let you know when we're ready to go in. Good luck to you all.'

There was a moment of silence in the loft. Then McGovern laughed his loud, hearty, Irish laugh, which always seemed somehow inappropriate for indoor use.

'Who was that masked man?' he said.

FORTY-TWO

*

It was goosing Cinderella time, around eleven forty-five, and I was reading McGovern's story in the *Daily News* for about the thirteenth time, pouring bullhorn-size portions of Jameson down my neck to settle my nerves, and communing with Sherlock's porcelain head and the cat. The lesbian dance class had ratcheted up in the loft overhead and that, as usual, made the cat a little edgy. Sherlock, however, continued to aim his logical hazel eyes directly at mine. His eyes remained unperturbed, intense, and slightly amused at how little the world had really changed. Mine, particularly after many medicinal rounds of Jameson, probably looked like two piss-holes in the snow. The only way I could know for sure would be to look in the mirror and the only mirror in the place was in the executive dumper, where I'd launched a large, rather fetid, nearly rhomboidal space station earlier that morning.

'Don't go in there without your hydrogen mask,' I said to the cat, while still perusing McGovern's column.

The cat, of course, said nothing. She had great disdain for any form of sophomoric, prepubescent, barnyard humor. She had, in fact, great disdain for any form of humor at all. It was really quite funny.

'You're a humorless, constipated prig,' I said to the cat.

The cat said nothing, but contented herself with switching her tail back and forth rather violently. It was, I thought, not so much a misunderstanding between a man and a cat. It was representative more of that intrinsic, deep-seated lack of trust that has always existed on some level between all men and all women. The cat looked at me with her logical hazel eyes. They remained unperturbed, intense, and slightly amused at how little the world had really changed.

McGovern's story about one devoted son's ceaseless search for his mother, to my mild surprise, had created a space station explosion of its own in New York. To those of us who knew Ratso, the pains and effort McGovern had gone through to portray him in a remotely attractive light seemed fairly amusing. McGovern's piece also provided great fodder for Don Imus and Howard Stern, the two New York-based radio titans who, as a rule, dumped on Ratso on a fairly regular basis. Now, both Imus and Stern, each after his own inimitable fashion, proceeded to dump on Ratso to a degree and an intensity that would've warmed the heart of Gustave Flaubert.

Neither knew, of course, that Ratso was in the sneezer. Nor did they know about the investigation or plan of attack that would soon be underway. Nor could they have any knowledge of the fact that if Mary Goodman wasn't living in a castle in Chappaqua, there weren't any cards left to play. Mary Goodman hadn't turned up in forty-seven years for a reason. No amount of press or publicity was going to bring her out of the woodwork at this late date. But it might've helped flush out Donald Goodman for the time being. However, there was no hard evidence on Goodman. None at all. Just a ridiculously skimpy circumstantial tissue of horseshit. Cecil Hausenfluck, a man who kicked his own ankles on a regular basis, had described Goodman to me. Travis Beaver, a tow-truck driver, had given me the name. His last name had matched the one I'd found in Jack Sloman's safe deposit box – the name of Ratso's birth mother. Then, of course, there was the matter of two dead bodies pointing vaguely to Goodman as the bad guy. But what, I thought, if Goodman was a bad guy but the wrong bad guy and Mary Goodman was no relation to him and she wasn't living in a castle in Chappaqua and there were no cards left to play?

'When there's no cards left to play,' I said to the cat, 'even destiny can't shuffle the deck.'

FORTY-THREE

I woke up the next morning with no scrotal-sarong difficulties but with something even more unpleasant. A poison dwarf was standing on the sidewalk four floors below my kitchen window screaming very personal slang obscenities at me in a piercing cockney accent. The last time I'd heard that kind of pathological timbre in a voice was when Cecil Hausenfluck had asked his mother if he was being rude. Mick Brennan, quite obviously, didn't care a bloody damn what anybody's mother thought.

'Put a sock in it, Mick,' I shouted, as I flung open the window and pitched the puppet head out into the feeble, freezing sunlight. Then I slammed the window back down and goose-stepped to the espresso machine, which I quickly cajoled into operation. Then I leaned against the kitchen counter, listened to it hiss and rattle, and waited for the inevitable.

'Goddamnit, mate,' said Brennan, as he roared in the door with the puppet head in one hand and a large envelope in the other, 'I've been up all bloody fucking night making these prints just so I could queue up and wait all bloody fucking morning for you to pop out of bed and toss me this bloody fucking puppet head.'

'Perhaps you would care for some tea,' I said in a conciliatory tone.

'Let's have a large helping of Jameson's, mate, and hold the bagels. Then we can look over these prints if you like.'

I poured a hefty shot of Irish whiskey into the bullhorn and handed it to Mick. I poured an equally hefty shot into my Imus in the Morning coffee mug, which I noticed had a little chip on its shoulder. So did I.

'Here's to your bloke Kent Perkins,' said Brennan, raising the bullhorn. 'I like him, and for all our sakes I hope he's not insane.'

'I'd say he's pretty damn clever stepping in in front of the security boys and telling the hired help to come back next week.'

We clinked our inappropriately stemmed receptacles and poured the Jameson down our necks.

'Always did believe in a hearty breakfast,' said Brennan.

'Okay, Mick, spit it. Did you get anything at all that would indicate that our little old lady may be in residence at the castle?'

'What'd you expect, mate? A double-parked aluminum walker? A close-up of her dentures smiling at you from the canasta table? I'm good but I'm not a bleeding spy satellite.'

With that proviso, Brennan slid the envelope over to me and slid himself in the direction of the door.

'I'm sure they'll prove invaluable,' I said, 'and we'll go over them very carefully before we move on the place. I was just hoping there'd be some sign of Mary Goodman. If she's not there, we can call in the dogs and piss on the fire.'

'Well, I hope we're not going in for nothing, mate. You told us Ratso's mother was there. You said you'd bet your life on it.'

'I'd still bet my life on it,' I said, as I placed the puppet head back on top of the fridge. 'I'm just wondering if the gods will be offering any odds.'

'They never have in the past, mate,' said Brennan, and he walked out the door.

That afternoon, with an imminent sense of D Day in the loft, I reviewed a small list of paint supplies as I waited for Stephanie DuPont to knock on my door. She was fashionably late. I used the time purposefully by returning a call to Mike Simmons at a new number he'd left on the machine.

'Good news,' he said, when he came on the line. 'Our new lawyer is not a piranha, he's a candiru. You know, the kind of thin little fish William Burroughs described in *Naked Lunch* that lives in the lower Amazon basin and darts up your ass or your prick and erects sharp spikes and can only be removed by surgery which, of course, is not feasible in the lower Amazon basin?'

'Was Burroughs writing from personal experience or was it just wishful thinking?'

'It was fishful thinking,' said Simmons. 'All I can tell you is that Ratso could be out of the can within twenty-four hours.'

'Allah be praised,' I said, more relieved than I might have sounded.

'Ratso seems very contrite. He knows he fucked up coming back to his apartment from Woodstock.'

'He's right.'

'He also says he should've told you in the beginning about the first detective he hired to find his mother.'

'He's right.'

'He also feels shitty because he's caused so much trouble for you and everybody else.'

'He's right again,' I said. 'Maybe there's something wrong with him.'

'Well,' said Simmons, 'we're all about to find out. He could be out on bail as early as tonight. I'm sure he'll call you and tell you all this stuff himself.'

'No doubt,' I said. 'I may be able to tell him something very soon, too. I may be able to tell him where Mary Goodman is. His mother.'

'That would make Ratso very happy.'

'Somehow I don't think Mary Goodman will quite derive the same enjoyment from this mother and child reunion.'

Later that afternoon I could see every head on Canal Street turning as Stephanie and I browsed the army-navy store circuit. None of the heads appeared to be looking at my cowboy hat.

'You're quite a hit on Canal Street,' I said.

'It's like this everywhere, ass brain,' said Stephanie. 'Or haven't you noticed?'

'Must be hard to manage,' I said, basking in the unbridled jealousy of every lowlife on the sidewalk.

'It's only hard to manage when I'm joined at the curvaceous hip by a Hebe detective nerd in a cowboy hat, smoking his hideous cigar.'

'Yeah,' I said understandingly. 'I know how that feels.'

We bought paint, brushes, white overalls, and white caps for Kent, McGovern, and myself. After some cajoling from Stephanie, I tried my outfit on in the store.

'You look like an orderly in a mental hospital,' Stephanie said, laughing.

'Not true,' I said. 'Only two professional groups always wear white caps. Rich men's sons and housepainters. I'm a housepainter.'

'I know,' said Stephanie wistfully.

'I appreciate your helping us with this surveillance,' I said, as we left the store with three large shopping bags. 'It could get a bit gnarly, you know.'

'Do you think it's a real castle?' she said with the sudden innocence of a near-child.

'I showed you Mick's pics of the place. Of course it's a real castle.'

'But just ask yourself: "If you were a real castle, would you live in Westchester?" '

'Probably not,' I said, as I unsuccessfully signaled a cab on Canal Street. 'But let's give the old castle a chance. You never know. Maybe you'll find your knight in shining armor.'

Stephanie raised her arm and a cab pulled immediately to the curb like a large, motorized puppet.

'You never know,' she said, tossing her head sharply and flailing her long blond hair halfway to Little Italy. 'Maybe we'll find Mary Goodman.'

FORTY-FOUR

Ratso didn't call. The cat and I had to content ourselves with the cold comfort of not knowing whether he was still in the sneezer or had been released on bail and was just pretending he didn't know us. For myself, I was too proud and too busy to bother with finding out. As far as the cat was concerned, she was too proud and too busy to bother with anything or anyone that did not directly please or intrigue her. If Ratso's life had depended upon it, she wouldn't have crossed the desk from one red telephone to the other. Cats are so clean.

As at least a grudging, time-share member of the wonderfully sensitive and complex human race, I feared I might be coming down with some spiritual malady akin to German measles and I did not wish for it to scar my conscience. Yes, I still planned to take my skilled team of secret agents out to the castle in the morning to find Ratso's mother. Yes, I'd already rather significantly risked life and limb, including several that didn't even belong to me, during the course of this investigation. I'd done for Ratso what Sherlock would've done for Watson or what Nero Wolfe would've done, albeit rather grudgingly, for Archie Goodwin. But I wasn't sure, now that I thought about it, that I'd ever really been a true friend to Ratso, whatever that meant.

In my more reflective moments, I had to admit that I was often rather hard on people, particularly those I liked to think of as my friends. Don't get me wrong. I was capable of kindness and acts of generosity toward others; it was just that something inside me always balked at thinking of myself in that way. What the hell, I thought. We are what we are if we're anything at all.

It was at about that time that I noticed the cat staring at me intently. Reading my ambivalent, meandering thoughts just as surely as she sucked the very breath from my body as she slept on my chest at night. It was a dangerous, vulnerable, almost frightening feeling. Like standing naked in front of the whole world. Or walking on the street in New York.

'So I'm human,' I said to the cat. 'What do you want from me?'

The cat said nothing, but continued to stare cryptically, like the oracle of Vandam.

'Okay, so maybe Kent Perkins *was* right,' I said. 'I'm a giver in a taker's body.'

The cat said nothing.

Suddenly I felt like Cecil Hausenfluck talking to a mother who wasn't there. I got up from the desk, poured a little nightcap of Jameson into the bullshorn, and took it over to the window where I killed the shot and gazed with level eyes across the fatuous, fourth-story neverness of the city night. A little soul-searching can always be forgiven, I thought, when you know that in the morning you're going to attack the castle.

FORTY-FIVE

*

Of course, we didn't really *attack* the castle. But if you've ever tried, you know that even merely insinuating yourself into a castle can be just about as dangerous. People who live in castles generally don't trust people who live outside castles. And they may have something there.

'Seems too easy, mate,' said Brennan the next morning as the five of us breakfasted on coffee and doughnuts in a nondescript rented van parked in front of a nearby Chappaqua diner.

'It *is* easy,' said Kent patiently.

'Just don't get caught,' added McGovern. He punctuated the comment with a machine-gun-like burst of highly infectious Irish laughter, which should've been illegal inside an enclosed van at eight o'clock in the morning.

'Most of the people working in and around the castle,' Kent continued, 'probably won't have been there much longer than us. When I checked earlier in the week there were a lot of new people, a number of temps, and a high turnover in general. That insures that nobody ever learns too much.'

'Yes,' said Stephanie, 'that's one way to look at it. But why permit people to crawl all over the place if you've got something or someone you've trying to hide?'

'I've pondered that one myself,' I said. 'It's a big operation to run an estate of this size and it'd look suspicious with no one ever around. Also, if Mary Goodman's there, or if she was there, the evidence may be limited to a small area inside the house. Donald Goodman's not going to be there anyway, so it's not a problem. But if he's got a crony or two watching over things, they certainly aren't threatened by what goes on outside the place. It may only become more dangerous, I suspect, if you have to go inside the house.'

'Comforting words for an interior decorator, mate,' said Brennan.

'Or the new French maid Donald Goodman hired,' said Stephanie.

'I was going to comment on that French maid outfit,' said Kent, 'but I was afraid God or Ruthie would strike me dead.'

'Now everybody just relax and look like you belong,' I said. 'Pretend you're in a strange neighborhood in the city. Just blend in. No one knows who Goodman may have hired or fired recently, so get your story down, keep it simple, and stick to it. And keep a look out for an old lady who may be closeted in a sun room or a little hidden garden somewhere.'

'Or a dungeon, mate.'

'Listen and observe,' I instructed, ignoring Brennan's remark. 'And be relaxed.'

'That's too much to remember,' said McGovern.

'By the time darkness falls on the castle,' said Kent Perkins dramatically, as he started the van's ignition, 'we'll have solved the mystery of Mary Goodman.'

As the van pulled out of the parking lot toward its date with destiny, each passenger, in his or her own way, seemed absorbed in placing the finishing touches on a new identity. I had to admit they looked the part. Now, if they could only act it.

'If you do meet your knight in shining armor somewhere in the castle,' I said to Stephanie, 'what do you plan to tell him?'

'Get in line,' she said.

Penetrating the grounds of the estate proved as easy as Kent had predicted, and was made even easier by the fact that every pair of male orbs in the place was totally zoning in on Stephanie DuPont in her French maid outfit. Quite possibly, we could've slipped the entire Polish Army into the front hall without anyone's being the wiser. And the front hall was just about big enough to accommodate the entire Polish Army.

The fortress was so large, indeed, that even Mick Brennan's surveillance photos had not done total justice to its magnitude nor its labyrinthine features. A body could get lost in here quite easily, I reflected, as I walked the lower floors unimpeded in my mental hospital drag, carrying a tape measure and a rather elaborate color chart. The fact was I'd already lost contact with everybody on our team except McGovern, the world's largest house painter, whom I could see through a set of stained-glass windows that would've made a Mormon missionary green with envy. McGovern was painting a forlorn-looking, frost-bitten little wooden garden trellis and he appeared to be enjoying his work. I found a side door and made my way over to him.

'I'm not sure,' I said, 'that a phlegm-colored trellis is exactly what they wanted here. When the spring greenery comes in, you're going to have a real clash problem.'

'That's okay,' said McGovern. 'By the time the spring greenery comes in I'll be gone.'

'McGovern, I want you to stay right here for as long as you possibly can. There's probably acres of woods and gardens on the place, but this spot provides a great overview of the house and the grounds. You may be the only chance we'll have to know where the hell the rest of us are. I'll come out periodically to reconnoiter on all movements other than bowel and to supervise the drying of your paint.'

'I can't paint this trellis forever,' said McGovern. 'What if some groundskeeper or security guy comes out and tries to fat-arm me?'

'You've got to stay put. This is also the only comprehensive view we have of what's going on inside the castle.'

'There's something now,' said McGovern, gesturing toward an upstairs window in the fortress-like structure.

We both looked up and saw a flash of blond hair sticking out from under a white painter's cap, as a large man who'd evidently been observing us stood up and turned around. Then a light-colored piece of cloth seemed to move downward out of our vision. Then, suddenly, in the window, apparently aimed directly at McGovern and myself, there appeared a pair of large, white, luminous buttocks.

FORTY-SIX

By Gary Cooper time, with our cover still holding nicely, we were able to swim around on the grounds and inside much of the castle in the blithe, practiced manner of the deadly candiru fish. The candiru, as Mike Simmons had gone on to explain, and as anybody who's ever urinated in the lower Amazon basin and lived to tell about it knows from empirical evidence, swims toward warmth. We, on the other fin, were swimming toward truth. And, as the afternoon wore on, our strokes grew bolder and stronger.

It soon became apparent that Perkins was correct about most of the servants and working people knowing less than we did. No one had seen an older lady on the premises, and the name Mary Goodman was usually responded to with a blank stare. There were, however, a few exceptions to this. One was an old man who looked like he'd been polishing silver in the scullery even longer than McGovern had been painting the trellis.

'Can you tell me where I can find Mary Goodman?' I asked him casually, as I went about comparing a nearby wall with my ever-present color chart.

'Oh, she's in her garden, sir,' he said, stopping his polishing almost imperceptibly, like a sleeping man pausing unknowingly before taking his next unconscious breath. 'She's not to be disturbed.'

'Where is her garden anyway?' I persisted.

'It's her private garden, sir. You'd have to check with Mr Goodman or Jennings.'

This posed somewhat of a problem, in that Mr Goodman, of course, was not on the premises and Jennings was obviously the head footman or Big Butler or somebody of such hierarchical stature that a mere housepainter like myself probably couldn't approach him with such a sensitive question. I wasn't sure how high up the ladder, as it were, I could climb.

As I thanked the old man I saw the reflection of my image in the silver plate he was polishing and I realized that one or both of us probably belonged in a mental hospital. I also realized that either Brennan or Stephanie would probably have to brace Jennings. If I were Jennings I would have given the guy in the silver plate the dust-off for sure.

I left to find Brennan, whom I'd seen about an hour before in all his sartorial splendor pushing the staff around like a little red apple. His personality was actually rather well suited for an interior decorator in a place like this, I thought. He could be as abrasive as he wished and everyone would still nod and bow and respectfully say: 'Yes, Mr Cunningham.' It was also refreshing to hear Brennan go through a whole morning without using the word 'mate'.

But Brennan was nowhere to be seen. Nor was Kent Perkins. Kent was a pro, however. He was the only one of us capable of casing the whole upstairs of the mansion and still find time to moon me and McGovern. The last time I'd seen Stephanie, she was chatting amiably with the old housekeeper and shooing me away with her hand when the woman wasn't watching. So, with the exception of Kent and Mick doing a disappearing act, the rest of our crew was fitting in so well it was beginning to make me nervous. As I remember, that was about the time things started to fall apart.

Suddenly, Brennan came running out of the house and grabbed my arm as I was attempting to light a cigar on a large veranda.

'Mate,' he said intensely, 'they're onto you.'

'Relax, Mick,' I said, with a confidence I did not particularly feel. 'You're behaving in a very un-interior-decorator-like fashion. Time may be running out for the housepainting crew – '

'It is. I overheard Jennings asking questions about the three of you.'

'But they're all still deferentially addressing you as "Mr Cunningham, sir" and Stephanie's got every pair of gonads on the grounds wrapped around her fingers with, of course, the possible exceptions of yours and mine and sometimes I'm not so sure about yours.'

'Mate, you'd better skate.'

'I don't think we'll have to. I doubt if Jennings knows for certain whether or not Goodman hired us. He's just got an enquiring mind. So do I and here's what I want you to do.'

I gave Mick a suggestion to pass along to Stephanie for me. It was nothing brilliant, really. Just an idea born of the times I'd lived my life around death.

Mick left to find Stephanie and I walked around the side of the house to see if McGovern was still at his command post. As I walked, I looked again to see where a private garden might be hiding itself, along with, of course, Mary Goodman. I searched for a good half an hour, but it was wintertime and it was hard to imagine what the place would be like in spring. Possibly, a private little winter garden might be tucked away somewhere on the sprawling grounds and Mary Goodman might be bundled up with her comforter on her divan sipping a hot camomile tea. There was also the possibility, I reflected, that just around the next corner, Judge Crater and Amelia Earhart might be busily pruning daffodils from the side lawn.

As I approached McGovern, Brennan's dire prediction seemed to be bearing its sour fruit. A large, armed security guard, almost as big as McGovern, was conversing with him in a manner that seemed far from congenial. I slowed my pace and was able to pick up the tail end of the conversation.

'On top of that, buddy,' said the burly security guard, 'this is the slowest fuckin' paint job I've ever seen.'

'This isn't a *paint* job,' said McGovern in a rather mincing, condescending whine. 'This is a *total surface restoration*.'

'We'll see about that,' said the guard, and he headed off toward the front of the house.

'I like that "total surface restoration",' I said, as I looked at my watch. 'I give our little housepainting crew about twenty minutes before they call in a forklift and get us out of here.'

'A lot can happen in twenty minutes,' said McGovern.

'And not all good,' I said. 'Here comes Kent.'

Kent Perkins was indeed approaching, looking slightly harassed and rubbing the knuckles on his right hand.

'Just had a minor altercation with a security guy,' he said, 'who won't be giving us any trouble for a while.'

'Unfortunately,' I said, 'there's about eighty-seven more of them crawling all over the place like so many burly praying mantises.'

'We're running out of time,' said McGovern, as he lazily slopped a few finishing touches on the phlegm-colored trellis. 'With nothing to show for it, I might add.'

'Not quite nothing,' said Kent with a quick smile. 'Stephanie got your message from Brennan and found this in the medicine cabinet in a disused boudoir upstairs.'

From his overalls pocket he extracted a plastic prescription bottle and held it in his palm for us to see. The name typed on the label was Mary Goodman. The date on the prescription was February 1984.

'Some of her effects, apparently, were still in the cabinet as well as other prescriptions, but, unfortunately, this was the most recent of the lot. She was definitely here, but it was over ten years ago.'

I puffed thoughtfully on my cigar and watched the cold sun shining on the mansion on the hill.

' "In last year's nests," ' I said, ' "there are no birds this year." '

'Who said that?' asked Kent.

'Don Quixote,' I said.

155

'That's about right,' said McGovern. 'I had a feeling we were tilting at windmills.'

'Not quite,' I said. 'Look over there.'

As we watched from our vantage point at the side of the castle, an evil baby blue Rolls Royce was rolling up the drive to the front door. We were able to see and not be seen, so we continued to watch the car as two men got out. The driver was Donald Goodman and he casually proceeded to walk into the house with the other man. When McGovern and I saw Goodman's companion, our faces must have reflected an astonishment roughly comparable to what we might have displayed at having just seen the Holy Ghost line-dancing on Country Music Television.

'Who was that?' asked Perkins.

Neither McGovern nor I answered until, after a moment, Kent must have figured it out for himself, because he didn't say anything either. We all just stood there like three fucked-up shepherds under a phlegm-colored trellis.

It was Ratso.

FORTY-SEVEN

*

Things moved at a breakneck pace after that. Perkins ran quickly toward the house, flattening himself against the outer wall and peering cautiously through a bay window into the great hall. McGovern and myself, not wishing to spook Ratso in a potentially dangerous situation, had to content ourselves with hiding behind a nearby hedge and watching Perkins watch Goodman. From our distant vantage point we could see dull images that we took to be Ratso and Goodman moving back and forth across our line of vision, occasionally coming very close to the window. Goodman appeared to be carrying some kind of shotgun or hunting rifle and showing it to Ratso.

'*Do you own a sawed-off shotgun, Tex?*'

'*Not to my knowledge.*'

The next thing I realized, McGovern was nudging me sharply in the ribs and Kent Perkins had discarded the paintbrush he'd been carrying and in his right hand he now held a gun. Then Goodman and Ratso disappeared from the window altogether and Perkins, in a scene vaguely reminiscent of Audie Murphy, ran toward us in a low crouch, still holding the gun, and jumped the small hedge, landing precariously close to my lit cigar.

'They're going hunting,' said Perkins.

'Well, fuck me gently with a chainsaw,' said McGovern.

'I overheard Ratso say: "I've never been pheasant hunting," ' said Kent. 'The problem is that for pheasant hunting you'd use something like a twenty-gauge and the shells would be six and a half birdshot.'

'So what's Goodman got?' I said. 'An elephant gun?'

'Damn close,' said Perkins. 'He's carrying a twelve-gauge shotgun and I could see the box of shells on the table. They're double-ought buckshot.'

'Which means?'

'Which means if they're hunting pheasant there's going to be nothing left to chew on.'

I chewed on the idea of Ratso going pheasant hunting with Donald Goodman and decided I didn't like it. I was just getting ready to figuratively spit it out when the back doors of the castle flung open and spit out the two great white hunters. Ratso was now carrying some kind of large burlap bag, presumably for the pheasant. Donald Goodman was still carrying the shotgun. They walked together into the woods.

'He's going to kill him,' said McGovern.

'He's sure going to *try*,' said Kent. 'I'm going after 'em.' And he did.

'McGovern,' I said, 'do you think you can get into the house and call the cops or the state police or somebody?'

'Sure,' said McGovern doubtfully. 'What do I tell them?'

'Tell them Mary Goodman's in the garden,' I said.

FORTY-EIGHT
*

I don't know if I could really *shoot* a pheasant,' came Ratso's rodent-like voice out of the womb of the woods.

'You may not get the chance,' said a deep, gravelly voice I took to be Goodman's. This was followed quickly by a short, surgical laugh, cold as the ground I was crawling on.

In fairness to Ratso, he'd been in the calaboose during all our efforts to track Goodman, so it stood to reason that he might fall prey to an invitation from his long-lost rich cousin to come up to the estate and be a country gentleman for a weekend. It was also fair to say that the fine art of social climbing was not lost on Ratso, and the opportunity to meet his mother, now that he suspected she was loaded, would draw him up here faster even than a hockey game.

At the moment, I couldn't see Ratso or Goodman and I didn't know where the hell Kent was. I wasn't even sure why I'd followed him into the woods. Without a weapon of my own, the only role I could play was to stay out of the way of Donald Goodman's buckshot.

I edged a little closer through the thick undergrowth until I heard the soul-splintering sound of a shell being pumped into the chamber of a shotgun. It was probably the last mortal sound that Bambi's mother ever heard, and it wasn't exactly music to my ears either. Then I heard it again. I crawled more quickly, ever closer to oblivion by obliteration, the only thought in my head being not to create the appearance of a large pheasant.

'You sure it's too cold for badminton?' asked Ratso. 'What does a pheasant look like anyway?'

'Pheasant?' Goodman laughed. 'Who said anything about a pheasant?' He laughed again. In the woods his laughter carried with a hollow, muffled, yet peculiarly penetrating sound, like the drums of death.

'Don,' said Ratso, a little unsure now, 'I thought you said we'd be hunting pheasant?'

I crawled closer. I could hear their voices quite clearly and what I heard was not reassuring.

'Pheasant?' said Goodman, who seemed to be playing with Ratso now. 'I didn't say we'd be hunting *pheasant*. I said it'd be *pleasant* to go hunting together. Do you know why?'

'Well, we *are* cousins,' said Ratso, now apparently clearly sensing that something was wrong. 'It's a good way to get to know each other. By the way, when is my mother getting here?'

'She's already here, cuz,' said Goodman, 'and you'll be meeting her soon. But we're not going to get to know each other, I'm afraid. We're just going to have a little hunting accident. Don't move or I'll kill you where you stand.'

Ratso, evidently, did not move. Neither did I. Their voices were almost on top of me now, it seemed, though through the undergrowth I could barely make out their images, like shadows in some poorly staged passion play. To move any closer, I thought, would be suicidal. So I listened, mesmerized by the deadly little scene, as if I were a creature of the wild, with nowhere to go and nowhere to stay, hypnotized by the very helplessness of being.

'It's like this, cuz,' Donald Goodman continued. 'Dear Aunt Mary and I lived very comfortably without a care in the world until the sweet old thing died about ten years ago. Of natural causes, I might add. I was so heart-broken I couldn't come to grips with the reality of dear Aunt Mary's death. So I just pretended she was still alive.'

'In other words,' said Ratso, 'you were keeping the goose that laid the golden egg even though you knew she was dead.'

'That's right, cuz,' said Donald Goodman, chuckling darkly in the dark forest. 'I like the way you pick up on things. Don't move. I mean it.'

There was an uncomfortable stillness in the woods. No birds. No animals. No Kent Perkins. Nothing but a silent shroud of sun-dappled darkness dancing its way downward to the forest floor.

'Oh, she was a strange bird, all right. I was her only known blood relation and I liked it that way. But dear Auntie had a will that she and her lawyers would never let me see. Of course, it doesn't matter now. She did speak of you now and again. She told me if God delivered her little David to her, everything she owned would be his. But I guess God didn't see it that way. He called her to her just reward long before you started hiring PIs and talking to lawyers and generally fucking things up. And now it's too late, cuz. Sorry we never got to know each other.'

There was a moment of silence almost like a silent prayer. Then came a desperate crashing of branches. Then a deafening blast. Then a bloodcurdling scream that seemed to die in the throat. Then another loud blast. Then nothing.

Nothing but the forest primeval.

FORTY-NINE
*

Three days later, a joint task force made up of the FBI and the New York State Police, using heat-sensing helicopters, infra-red cameras, and cadaver dogs, located the body of Mary Goodman. She was in the garden. Interestingly enough, her remains were found not far from a curious-looking phlegm-colored trellis that seemed to stand a silent vigil over the entire operation. The joint task force, though disinclined to get involved with the murders of Jack Bramson and Moie Hamburger, had been keeping a close eye on Donald Goodman for what they deemed to be more important reasons – money laundering and federal tax fraud. To this end, they had infiltrated both Goodman's corporation and his estate near Chappaqua. The guard, for instance, that had tried to fat-arm McGovern had been working undercover for the New York State Police.

This did not surprise me nearly as much as the news I heard from Kent Perkins almost a week to the day after he'd blown away Donald Goodman. The head of the entire joint task force was a federal agent working undercover who'd been on Goodman's payroll for over eight months. The agent directing the operation was, according to Perkins, an older man who spent much of his time polishing silver plates.

Kent, incidentally, spent several days under the shadow of arrest for killing Donald Goodman with a weapon that was unlicensed in the state of New York. He was rather stoic about the whole ordeal, however, reciting to me what he said was the cop's routine rejoinder in situations of this nature. 'I'd rather be tried by twelve,' Kent had said, 'than carried by six.' As it evolved, of course, neither was necessary, and Kent Perkins, a job well done, was able to return to California, thereby repopulating that state with one more large, attractive, blond person.

Ratso, who suffered only a grazing wound to his left buttock, now stands, at this writing, to inherit slightly under fifty-seven million dollars. From this windfall, as might be expected, there will have to be extracted rather sizable legal fees that have been engendered by Ratso's having retained a candiru-like phalanx of lawyers that has, as also might be expected, become too sated with treading water in his prospective reservoir of riches to swim either toward warmth or truth.

To his credit, Ratso did leave a message on my answering machine that fateful day, telling me he was going out pheasant hunting with his new cousin. The cousin, according to Ratso, had read McGovern's piece in the *Daily News* and was making arrangements as well for Ratso to soon get together with his mother. Once Ratso was out on bail, of course, Goodman would know exactly how to get in touch with him at his apartment. He'd already killed him there once. Now, he realized, time was running out for him to eliminate this threat to his inheritance once and for all. And he moved very quickly. Goodman had also, apparently, been alerted to Ratso's quest on the radio. It isn't clear, however, at this writing, whether he'd heard it on Don Imus or on Howard Stern.

Unfortunately, I was already in Chappaqua when Ratso had called, having left the cat in charge of the loft. The cat, for whatever her reasons, failed to give me the message.

One final and rather disturbing note on Ratso. He has determined, for whatever his reasons, that his many new friends, as well as his relatively few older ones, should address him as David Victor Goodman. He is having very little success with this campaign and, I'm afraid, he's taking it all rather personally. I've counseled him that patience will win the day and that soon people will relate to his newfound identity as readily as they now appear to relate to his newfound wealth. Privately, however, I fear this will not be the case. It is a troubling but true phenomenon of life that people who, for whatever the reason, possibly through no fault of their own, have assumed animal names, invariably find them impossible to shed for all eternity. So if you are indeed saddled with one of these names, you may consort with the Rockefellers, but you will forever be a Ratso.

FIFTY
*

About three weeks later, back at the loft one afternoon, much in the manner of men in mental hospitals, I put on my white housepainter's cap and read to the cat a portion of a letter I'd recently received from Lilyan Sloman. Ratso by now had told her about the death of his birth mother and, apparently, a few other things as well.

' "You will never know," ' she says, ' "how much I appreciate what you've done for Larry." '

'That's nice,' I said. The cat, evidently, did not agree, for she switched her tail violently from side to side and stared stonily away in the opposite direction.

' "I know that you, too, have lost your mother fairly recently," ' I continued reading, ' "and I'm sure this did not make the search any easier for you. I only wanted to tell you the same thing I told Larry. No one can ever take the place of a person's real mother. But sometimes there are other places." '

'Sometimes there are other places,' I said to myself, and the cat, now that I wasn't addressing her directly, seemed to pick up my mood. She stopped thrashing her tail and crawled into my lap.

'Who knows,' I said. 'Maybe one of those places is right here in this loft.'

That night I dreamed I was driving a Rolls Royce across a vivid landscape in a tropical clime. In the front seat with me were Robert Louis Stevenson and Uncle Rosie. It was a beautiful day and everyone was smiling as we drove along an endless road under a swaying canopy of palm trees that seemed at once to belong to the sea and the sky.

Into this idyllic occasion was suddenly injected a strange thunking sound accompanied at irregular intervals by a not entirely unpleasant vibration in the area of my buttocks. This disruption continued for some miles until Robert Louis Stevenson turned around and peered deeply into the backseat of the Rolls.

'I say, old man, this *is* quite odd,' said the great author. 'There appears to be a small Aryan child kicking the back of your seat.'

In the morning, I lit my first cigar of the day and called Dr Charles Ansell, an old friend of my father's and a pre-eminent world expert on the analysis of dreams. I told Charlie the dream. I also told him that I rather suspected that the highway upon which we were traveling was the Road of the Loving Hearts.

'I can only analyze a dream,' said Charlie, 'in relation to a specific person and his or her experiences. But I can tell you a few quick points that seem to be indicated here. For instance the Rolls Royce. The wish explains the dream. You wish to give the appearance of a guy entitled to a Rolls Royce. And the palm trees. They grow tall, stiff, and erect. A palm tree is as near to a phallic reference as anything you can dream about.'

'So far,' I said, 'so good.'

'Uncle Rosie. Was he your uncle?'

'No.'

'Then he's the uncle everybody wishes he could've known better.'

'Charlie, you're readin' my mail.'

'A dream is more revealing than any form of conscious intercourse. Now what about Robert Louis Stevenson? You liked *Treasure Island*?'

'*Dr Jekyll and Mr Hyde.*'

'This is a dream analysis, not psychoanalysis. Now the small Aryan child is a problem. At first I thought he might be you, but now I think he's determined to always stand in the way of your complete happiness. His destiny is to keep you miserable. But did he inherit this role? Was he inoculated as a baby? How does he know you're a Jew? Is your other imaginary car a Mercedes? Anyway, if the kid comes back, let me know.'

'If the kid comes back I may be calling from the Pilgrim State Mental Hospital.'

'No, seriously,' said Charlie, 'it's a dream of great hope for the future. Especially the palm trees. I like the palm trees.'

'They speak very highly of you.'

'By the way, this place you describe – what is it? – lovely name – '

'The Road of the Loving Hearts?'

'That's it,' said Charlie. 'But the question I have for you is this: Do you actually know whether or not this road really exists?'

I took a measured puff on the cigar and then the cat and I watched the blue smoke drift dreamily upward toward the lesbian dance class.

'Charlie,' I said, 'you tell me.'

ACKNOWLEDGEMENTS

*

Dear Occupant:

The author would like to express his deep gratitude to all the people who've helped him in his life, including those who have died and gone to Jesus, many of whom have reported that He looks a little like Andy Gibb. As far as the living are concerned, and you know who you are, thanks for the Hawaiian coffee, the Cuban cigars, the encouragement, and, in some cases, the valid criticism. The author does not take valid criticism well and it often causes him to become highly agitato, plunging him into prolonged periods of petulance and pique, not to mention alliteration. All this notwithstanding, much of the blame must be placed squarely on the shoulders of the usual suspects:

Esther 'Lobster' Newberg, literary agent par excellence, who loves me more than she loves anyone except Ted Williams and Bobby Kennedy. 'The Kinkster will soon be fartin' through silk,' says Lobster;

Chuck Adams, editor extraordinaire, who knows what to leave in, what to take out, and when to take a spiritual rain check. After months of working intensely with Jackie Collins, Charlton Heston, and myself, Chuck is now going over manuscripts at the Bandera Home for the Bewildered;

Don Imus, who got me with Esther, got me with Chuck, and got me expert medical advice many years ago when I noticed several drops of blood in my semen. Upon observing this singular phenomenon, I called Imus to say goodbye. I was, quite naturally, convinced that the date on my carton had expired. That, however, was not to be the case. The Baby Jesus, who, I understand, looks a little like Winston Churchill, wanted me to live so I could share this rather poignant personal experience with you, Gentile Reader. Imus's doctor merely prescribed that I refrain from overly zealous, Dylan Thomas-like self-gratification for at least two weeks. I complied, and was eventually able to whip my illness. Imus, of course, continues to maintain a seminal role in my life.

I'd also like to thank some very important British people with whom I have professional intercourse on a fairly regular basis. None of them has brought me grief. Yet. They are as follows: Robert McCrum for discovering me; Joanna Mackle for launching me; Matthew Evans for nuturing me in matters beyond the coin of the spirit; Angela Smith for feeding me, and a special thanks to Anthony Wall for getting the show on the road.

Also a tip of the old Yamaha on my head to Deborah Rogers for playing such an integral part in helping to make the Kinkster an international household nerd.

And finally, before these acknowledgements begin to cut into my cocktail hour, I'd like to pass along a bare snippet from a rather illuminating conversation I had last week with the gorgeous Stephanie DuPont. She was in the process of reading out loud to me from an article in what she calls her bible and what the rest of us call *People* magazine. The newsflash concerned one of the members of the band U2 who'd recently forsaken his palatial rock-star residence and moved, with all attendant publicity, into a lighthouse.

'What do you think, banzai dick?'

'Waste of a lighthouse,' I said.